'I thought blondes were supposed to be cool and unemotional.'

Wolf studied Lydia's angry face with a superior frown.

'Mr Strade, I——' She stopped abruptly as hot colour flooded her pale, creamy skin.

'The name's Wolf.'

Lydia glared at him. For some strange reason her body was determined to be aroused by a man she both disliked and disapproved of. But he was so cold, so self-contained. Didn't *anything* touch him?

Kids…one of life's joys, one of life's treasures.

Kisses…of warmth, kisses of passion, kisses from mothers and kisses from lovers.

In *Kids & Kisses*…every story has it all.

Helen Brooks lives in Northamptonshire and is married with three children. As she is a committed Christian, busy housewife and mother, her spare time is at a premium but her hobbies include reading, swimming, gardening and walking her two energetic, inquisitive and very endearing young dogs. Her long-cherished aspiration to write became a reality when she put pen to paper on reaching the age of forty and sent the result off to Mills & Boon.

Recent titles by the same author:

LOVERS NOT FRIENDS
ANGELS DO HAVE WINGS
DARK OASIS
LACE AND SATIN

FIRE BENEATH THE ICE

BY

HELEN BROOKS

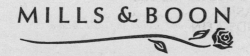

MILLS & BOON

All the characters in this book have no existence outside the imagination of the author, and have no relation whatsoever to anyone bearing the same name or names. They are not even distantly inspired by any individual known or unknown to the author, and all the incidents are pure invention.

*MILLS & BOON and the Rose Device
are trademarks of the publisher.
Harlequin Mills & Boon Limited,
Eton House, 18-24 Paradise Road, Richmond, Surrey TW9 1SR
This edition published by arrangement with
Harlequin Enterprises B.V.*

© Helen Brooks 1995

ISBN 0 263 79070 3

*Set in Times Roman 10 on 12 pt.
01-9508-57779 C1*

Made and printed in Great Britain

CHAPTER ONE

'I HOPE you haven't got me another empty-headed little bimbo out there, Connoly, who is more interested in a chip in her nail varnish than getting on with the damn job.'

'Mr Strade——'

'I told you my requirements last night and I meant what I said. Grey hair, middle-aged, with nothing less than a first-class typing speed and skirts down to her ankles, OK?'

'Please, Mr Strade——'

Lydia found her mouth had fallen open in a little O of shocked surprise as she stood waiting in the outer office where Mr Connoly had positioned her thirty seconds before. He had smiled at her apologetically before scuttling into the inner sanctum of the chairman and managing director of Strade Engineering, motioning for her to stay where she was until he returned. He had obviously intended to shut the door, but it had opened the merest crack after he had closed it and now the conversation of the two men inside was clearly audible.

'You changed the agency?' the hard masculine voice continued grimly.

'Yes, Mr Strade.' She could just imagine Mr Connoly's thin, nervous face trying to smile. 'Of course. But you must understand that it was such short notice that most of their employees were already in a position.'

'And that means?'

'This lady is extremely capable, I do assure you, and I'm sure she will meet all your work requirements admirably.' The nervous squeak wouldn't have convinced Lydia, and clearly Mr Strade was of the same opinion.

'She isn't a blonde-haired bombshell, is she?' the harsh voice asked tightly. 'It's going to be another few months before Mrs Havers comes back after this damn maternity leave, and already I've endured two females who were a darn sight more interested in the size of my bank balance than doing the job they were hired for. Short skirts and fluttering eyelashes have their time and place, but my office is not one of them. Are you sure this one isn't on the make?'

Enough was enough. The flood of anger that burnt hotly through Lydia's pale, creamy skin brought her small chin militantly upwards and made her deep brown eyes shoot sparks. Who on earth did this creep think he was? Robert Redford and Richard Gere rolled into one? She had pushed open the door and stepped into the huge plush room beyond before she had time to consider what she was going to say.

'Do excuse the interruption, gentlemen,' she said coolly, her eyes sweeping in magnificent disdain over the two men standing by the far window, 'but in view of your conversation, I hardly think there is any point in my waiting any longer. I'll see myself out.' The sunlight streaming in through the panoramic plate glass held the two men in silhouette, although one was clearly taller and broader than the other and it was to this figure that she addressed the last remark. 'Do have a good day, Mr Strade,' she finished with acid sweetness as she turned to leave.

'Stay exactly where you are.' She didn't even think about disobeying him; there was something in the deep voice that demanded and received acquiescence, although her chin raised itself another notch as she swung round to face the two men again. As they moved from the window and into focus she was aware of two thoughts striking her simultaneously, both of which were acutely unwelcome in the circumstances. One was that the tall figure just in front of Mr Connoly was hopping mad, if the scowl on his dark face was anything to go by, and the other? The other was that he was the most attractive man she had seen for a long time. She hadn't been far wrong with the Robert Redford and Richard Gere comparison, she thought weakly as he came to a halt just in front of her, his six-foot frame seeming to dwarf her slim, petite five feet four.

'Yes?' She raised her eyes to meet the arctic blue of his, her face straight. He had been rude, incredibly, unforgivably rude, and if he thought she was going to crawl now he'd soon find out differently.

'What the hell do you mean by bursting into my office uninvited?' he asked cuttingly, his eyes moving to her ash-blonde hair, secured in a neat and demure French plait at the back of her head, with more than a touch of resigned contempt in the blue gaze.

'Blonde-haired bombshell'. The words spoken with such raw harshness came back to her. Well, she had blonde hair, that much was for sure, and she'd die before she apologised for the fact, especially to a male chauvinist pig like this one.

'Don't be so ridiculous, Mr Strade,' she said coolly, blessing the impulse that had made her wear her best suit that morning instead of the usual blouse and pencil-slim skirt she favoured. The expensive material and beautiful cut of the suit always made her feel good, and she had felt, after the agency had rung, that she might need something of a boost if she was stepping into the domain of such an illustrious and well-known mogul as Strade of Strade Engineering. Little had she known then how right she was! 'I did not burst into your office, as you are well aware. The door was open and I had been asked to wait just outside, where every word of your conversation with Mr Connoly was received loud and clear. In view of the fact that I only qualify on one of the requirements you laid out in such graphic detail, I assumed there was no point in my continuing to wait.'

'And that is?' he asked coldly. The frown had died now, to be replaced by an expression of almost blank coolness.

'My typing speed.' It was hard work to keep her gaze from faltering from the rapier-sharp eyes, but she was determined to hang on in there. 'My hair is blonde, I am twenty-seven years of age and my skirt——' she glanced down for just a second to the tapered material that finished just below her knees '—is not ankle-length,' she finished tightly.

'No...' His eyes had followed hers and lingered for just a second on the length of slender leg encased in gossamer-thin stockings the skirt exposed. 'No, it isn't.' As the icy gaze met hers again she found it hard to stop a shiver from showing. There was a coldness in his eyes, his whole face, that was positively raw in its bleakness, turning the high, chiselled cheekbones and square, hard jaw into stone. He had to be the most detached, unapproachable man she had ever met in her whole life. And the two girls before her had made a pass at this block of ice? She'd like to shake their hands for sheer nerve.

'Goodbye, then, Mr Strade.' She hadn't even begun to turn this time when the frosty voice rang out again.

'*I* do the hiring and firing, and as yet I am not aware that either applies. You came for an interview and my time is valuable and not to be wasted. Sit down, Miss...?'

'I'd rather not.' She didn't know where this aplomb was coming from—perhaps the chill that was emanating from him was affecting her, because in all fairness she should feel grossly intimidated, but instead her cheeks were burning with rage. 'And it's Worth, *Mrs* Worth,' she finished with cold emphasis.

'You're married?' The relief on his face was transparent and added to Lydia's sense of outrage. What did he expect her to do, for goodness' sake? Leap over the desk and rip off his trousers at the slightest encouragement? The man's ego was jumbo-sized.

'Yes, but I really don't think——'

'Please sit down, Mrs Worth.' The transformation was sudden and breathtaking. What had been a block of stone metamorphosed instantly into the secretary's ideal of the perfect boss—smiling, handsome and exuding benevolence. 'We seem to have got off on the wrong foot, for which I accept the blame entirely.'

It was a twenty-four-carat smile, she had to give him that, Lydia thought weakly as she felt herself persuaded into the large, easy seat opposite the magnificent shiny desk in gleaming walnut. Mr Connoly still continued to hover anxiously at his managing director's side, his mild, watery eyes begging her to be reasonable.

'Could we put this unfortunate episode aside and begin anew?' The vivid blue eyes fastened on her again and she realised with a little jolt that they were still as hard as iron. She had read somewhere that the eyes were considered windows to the soul in some cultures, and if that were the case... The shiver returned tenfold. 'I don't know how much Mr Connoly has told you about the position, but my very able and efficient secretary is at present on maternity leave.' The harsh twist to his mouth as he spoke revealed his opinion of the poor woman's amazing audacity more eloquently than any words could have done. 'The agency we were with until yesterday provided ... unsuitable replacements, and I do not have the time or the inclination to continue along that particular avenue.' His scathing comments on her predecessors returned with renewed vigour and she nodded non-committally as her mind raced.

'I want a secretary for the next few months who is prepared to work hard and be flexible when the occasion warrants it,' he continued coldly. 'Mrs Havers was forced to leave a month early due to some unforeseen difficulties, so I have been left in rather a vulnerable position, and I don't like that, Mrs Worth.' His smile was ironic. 'I don't like that at all.' She glanced again at the firm, cruel mouth and ruthless, handsome face and nodded mentally. She could believe that, very definitely. She didn't smile back.

'For the right person, the rewards will match the dedication I require,' he said quietly, after waiting a moment for her to speak, 'but you understand this is not a nine-to-five job.'

As Mr Connoly opened his mouth to speak, the other man glanced at him, motioning towards the door with a hard flick of his wrist. 'Coffee, I think, Ted? Perhaps you'd organise that?' he asked coldly.

'Certainly, certainly.' Mr Connoly fairly scampered across the room and out of the door, clearly glad to be out of a potentially difficult situation.

'Mr Strade, I don't think——'

He cut across her voice as though he hadn't heard her, his tone reasonable, but with that underlying thread of steel that made her hackles rise. 'The salary is not the usual agency rate, but if you accept the position you will earn every penny.' He mentioned a figure that made her eyes widen and her mouth open slightly before she closed it with a little snap. With that amount guaranteed even for two or three months, she could afford to redecorate Hannah's bedroom, turning it from a nursery into a little girl's room, and perhaps even lash out on a new carpet for the lounge—the other *was* threadbare. And definitely those outstanding bills wouldn't keep her awake any longer at night. But to work in close contact with this man each and every day? Could she endure it?

'Of course, you may feel that, with family commitments, you couldn't accept such a post if it was offered.'

'I'm sorry?' She raised her head from mental calculations of gas, electricity and water bills, realising she hadn't heard a word he'd said in the last thirty seconds.

'Your husband,' he said patiently, his face expressionless. 'Perhaps he would object to you working late or having to take off at short notice for a couple of days? It is not unusual for me to have to visit my subsidiaries at an hour's notice and, as I have branches in Scotland, Wales, Manchester and Ireland, it often necessitates an overnight stay. Some husbands would find this unacceptable.'

Now was the moment to tell him. She stared across the desk into the austere face opposite her, but images of pink frilly curtains and flowery bedspreads and Hannah's little face came between. If she told him she was a widow, she would be out of the door before she could say Jack Robinson, she thought frantically. He would think she was available, or at least that she thought *he* was available, she corrected mentally. And she knew that he was the last person on this earth she could harbour any romantic inclinations for, so where was the harm in a little unspoken deceit? And she wouldn't *actually* lie, not really. And she needed that money, desperately. The mortgage had been paid off after Matthew's death but the old, draughty terraced house ate gas and electricity, and the last three years had been an uphill struggle to survive on what she could earn. If her mother, herself a widow, hadn't insisted on helping out as unpaid child-minder, financial waters would have closed over her head more than once...

'Mrs Worth?' Now the hard, deep voice was clearly impatient. 'Would your husband find unsocial hours unacceptable?' he asked tightly.

'No.' She raised her head and stared him straight in the eye. 'No, he wouldn't,' she answered firmly.

'Good.' He settled back on the corner of the desk where he was perched, looking down at her. 'Then perhaps this might be the time for a short test of your skills. You do do shorthand as well as audio-typing?'

'Yes.' She slipped a hand down to her bag and brought out notebook and pencil. 'When you're ready.'

Half an hour later, as she presented a neatly typed, well-set out report in front of him, he glanced up from his desk, his eyes narrowed. 'Sit down, Mrs Worth.' He flicked through the pages quickly and nodded slowly. 'Excellent. The job is yours if you want it.'

'I...' *Did* she want it? She glanced down at his lowered head, noticing the gleam of red in his black hair—virile, thick, strong hair. Her stomach muscles clenched in an involuntary spasm she was at a loss to understand. No, she was suddenly quite sure she didn't want the job if it entailed being close to this man for a few hours every day, but she *did* want the money, No, not want, *need*.

'Well?' The icy blue gaze was suddenly fixed on her flushed face and she took a deep silent breath as she struggled for composure.

'Thank you, Mr Strade,' she said levelly. 'I would like the job, please.'

'Good.' His eyes lowered to the papers on his desk that he had been studying when she had entered the room from the secretary's office just beyond. 'Go and get yourself a cup of coffee and a sandwich and make any phone calls you think necessary; you'll be working late tonight. I've a hell of a lot of work to catch up on.'

He hadn't asked if she had any children, she thought bemusedly as she left the room. Hadn't it occurred to him?

She had just reached the desk in the outer office when the buzzer on the intercom sounded stridently, making her jump a mile. 'Yes?' As she flicked the switch she was annoyed to find her voice a little breathless.

'I forgot to ask.' His voice was uncompromisingly severe. 'Are there any little Worths?' She knew what he wanted her answer to be, and it would be easy to lie, but somehow she couldn't deny Hannah's presence in her life, even if it meant losing this golden opportunity for the pair of them to get on their feet.

'Yes.' She kept her voice steady and clear. 'I have a daughter aged three, Mr Strade.'

'Oh.' She could tell he had expected a denial. 'You have an understanding child-minder?' he asked coolly.

'Hannah is looked after by my mother when I'm at work, and she is very flexible. The hours will be no problem.' She could feel her heart thudding as she waited for his reply. Suddenly the amount of money he was offering was desperately important. 'She's a widow and likes the company,' she added quietly.

'Be back in the office by twelve, Mrs Worth.' The flick of a switch signalled the end of their conversation and she stared at the closed door of his office as her heartbeat returned to normal. He really was the original ice-man but... She sank down on the upholstered typist's chair at the smart desk as her thoughts raced on. He *had* given her a chance and she was honest enough to admit that quite a few men in his position would have hesitated in taking on a secretary with a young daughter in tow, however temporary the position, in view of the travelling and long hours the job entailed.

She was back in the outer office within half an hour of leaving it, after a brief explanatory phone call to her mother, who responded with maternal encouragement, after which Lydia gulped a hasty cup of coffee in the splendid canteen and decided against one of the delicious meals on offer. She bought a pack of ham sandwiches to eat later—she was far too nervous to eat anything now in spite of having skipped breakfast once the agency rang—and returned to the thickly carpeted, hushed opulence of the top floor. The grandeur of the huge building had begun to get through to her, and the fact that she was working for a multimillionaire who could buy and sell half of London if he so chose was more than a little awe-inspiring.

It wasn't that she didn't think she could handle the job, she thought feverishly as she opened the drawers of her desk to familiarise herself with the contents, it was just... Just what? she asked herself irritably. What on earth was the matter with her? Since Matthew's untimely death from undiagnosed genetic heart disease just a few weeks after Hannah was born, she had kept both herself and her tiny daughter, as well as running a home and coming to terms with the emotional package of grief and anger her loss had entailed. So why was she letting an ice-cold individual like Mr Strade get to her? It was ridiculous. *She* was ridiculous! She nodded mentally and took a few deep, calming breaths as she forced her heartbeat to behave. She was mature and sensible and perfectly in control of her emotions and her life, not some giddy schoolgirl with no responsibilities and no brain.

'You're back already?' She came out of her reverie abruptly as a cool voice spoke from the doorway, and raised her eyes to meet the direct blue gaze trained on her face. 'Ready for work?'

'Of course, Mr Strade.' She smiled mechanically as she tried to keep her nervousness from showing. She could understand why those girls before her could have been initially attracted to him—he really was an absolute dish—but surely within ten minutes of meeting him those ice-blue eyes would have frozen over even the most ardent female heart? She had never met a less approachable man in her life.

'Wolf.'

'What?' She forgot to be polite as she stared at him open-mouthed.

'We are going to be working in close contact for a ridiculous number of hours a day, so I suggest we drop the formality,' he said coolly. 'I understand your first name is Lydia?' She nodded weakly. 'And mine is Wolf.'

'It is...?' She really wasn't handling this very well, she thought miserably as she watched the hard mouth tighten at her reaction. It was perfectly clear he had had this conversation more times than he would have liked in his life, but with a Christian name like that it was hardly surprising! She stared at him as she tried to pull herself together. And when added to his appearance and whole demeanour——

'My father was a wild-life expert involved in an expedition studying the Canadian timber-wolf at the time of my birth,' he said coldly, after a few uncomfortable seconds had ticked by. 'Unfortunately he thought the name rather apt for his baby son and my mother did little to dissuade him.'

'Oh.' She blinked tensely. 'You haven't got a middle name, have you?' she asked tactlessly.

A glimmer of a smile touched the hard mouth for an instant as he turned away. 'Fortunately, no. I hardly dare think what that would have been. Now, if you'd care to bring your notebook...?'

What an incredibly stupid thing to say, Lydia, she berated herself fiercely as she followed him into the massive office a moment later. The little incident had been a perfect opportunity to impress him with her diplomacy and discreet delicacy, and all she had managed was, 'You haven't got a middle name, have you?' She cringed mentally.

'Do stop looking so tragic.'

'What?' For the second time in as many minutes, he took her completely by surprise and it showed.

'In spite of my name, I really don't eat little girls for breakfast, especially when they look like you,' he added surprisingly as the shuttered gaze passed remotely over her clear, creamy, translucent skin in which the dark brown of her heavily lashed eyes stood out in startling contrast to the ash-blonde of her hair. 'Your colouring is most unusual.'

'It's natural.' She raised a defensive hand to her hair, sensing criticism as her mind flew back to the remarks he had made on her predecessors.

'I'm sure it is,' he said gravely, without a glimmer of amusement in either his face or voice, although she felt, somehow, that that was exactly what he was feeling. 'Now, do you think you could relax a little? We've one hell of an afternoon in front of us and it would be a great help if you could ease up a little.'

She nodded tightly as anger replaced the nerves. He really did have the most colossal cheek! She wouldn't be feeling like this if he had been halfway to normal. Something of what she was thinking must have shown on her face because the quirk to his mouth was definitely wry as he lowered his gaze to the papers on his desk. 'Right, then, if you are ready?'

She was conscious, somewhere towards evening, of being utterly astounded at the speed and energy with which Wolf Strade devoured the workload in front of him, despite a hundred and one interruptions every two minutes and numerous telephone calls for which she, at least, was pathetically grateful. It gave her a chance to check her frantic shorthand and get her thoughts in order for the next barrage.

The September evening was growing dark outside when she walked dazedly from his office a few hours after entering it, with a small list of several items of correspondence he needed typing before she left. She sat down at her desk with a weary little plop and flexed her aching hand gently. He was some sort of a machine! She stared across at the closed door separating them, aware that her head was pounding, and a distinct feeling of nausea was reminding her that she hadn't eaten all day. Well, she had no time now: it was going to be at least another two hours before she could leave——

'Lydia?' The box on her desk crackled as it spoke her name abruptly. 'Order us both coffee and sandwiches and take a break for half an hour. You're no good to me looking like you did when you left this room.'

'I'm fine.' She glared at the inoffensive intercom as Wolf's last words made her cheeks burn. 'I can——'

'Do as you are told.' The tone was uncompromising. 'I rarely make suggestions—that was an order, in case you didn't recognise it.' Both the harshness of the deep voice and the authoritative arrogance made her hands clench at her sides as she struggled for composure, but it was a good few seconds before she could bring herself to reply. How was she going to stand working for this megalomaniac for five or six days, let alone five or six months?

'Very good, Mr Strade.' The use of his surname was deliberate and there was a blank silence for a moment before he spoke again.

'Did you come by car this morning?' he asked coldly. She nearly said 'What?' for the third time that day and checked herself just in time. 'No, I didn't,' she said abruptly. 'I travelled by tube—it's not far.'

'Then when we're finished here you order a taxi. The name of the firm we use is under T in Mrs Havers's address-book in the left-hand drawer of the desk, and you charge to the firm's account, OK?'

'There's really no need——'

The deep, long-drawn out sigh cut short her protest. 'I might have known.' His voice was laconic and extremely sarcastic. 'Here was I thinking I'd found the perfect substitute secretary—pleasant to look at, highly efficient and utterly devoid of fanciful ideas.' By that she supposed he meant that with a husband and child in evidence he was safe, she thought furiously. 'But unless I'm very much mistaken, there is a strong streak of stubbornness in you, Mrs Lydia Worth. Would you really prefer to wander about London on your own late at night when you can be safely transported to your door?'

'I don't intend to wander anywhere,' she retorted tightly, 'but I am more than capable of getting home——'

'Order the taxi ten minutes before you think you've finished,' he said sharply, 'and I don't want to hear another word on the subject.' She heard him mutter something rude a moment before the click of the intercom signalled the conversation was at an end.

She wasn't going to be able to stand this. She shut her eyes for a second before lifting the internal phone to call down to the canteen for the coffee and sandwiches. He had to be the epitome of all the qualities she most disliked in the male of the species, he really did. It wasn't so much what he said but the way he said it most of the time—arrogance was far too weak a word to cover such cold, aggressive hostility. Was he like this all the time?

She was pondering exactly the same uncomfortable thought later that night as she lay in the peace and tranquillity of her bedroom with her head spinning from the impressions of the day. She had finished the work he wanted just before eight, presenting the neat pile of typewritten pages to him in fear and trepidation and waiting by the side of his desk while he checked them through.

'Excellent.' He had raised piercing blue eyes to the soft brown of hers. 'I can see we are going to get along fine, Lydia, despite a few hiccups. Have you ordered the taxi?' She had nodded reluctantly and his mouth had twitched as he lowered his eyes to his desk again. 'Good. Well I suggest you scoot off home to that husband of yours and reassure him that this won't happen every night. Goodnight.'

'Goodnight.' She had just reached the door when his voice had spoken her name again.

'And, Lydia?' She had turned to face him, her eyes apprehensive. 'You really have done a magnificent job today, thank you.' And then he had smiled, really smiled, and she had almost reeled from the shock of it, from the transformation it had wrought on his whole face.

Had he smiled at those other girls like that? she asked herself as she flexed her toes in the warmth from the electric blanket—it was almost October now and had been a particularly cold autumn. If so, she could understand why they had been smitten. Not that it affected her like that, she assured herself hastily, definitely not. She knew what he was really like—cold, aloof, hard and quite inexorable, but nevertheless ... The softening of the austere classical features would cause any female's heart to give a little jump.

Thank goodness she was immune. She nodded to herself firmly. He was pleased with her because she did her job well and was guaranteed not to get any romantic ideas about him. Well, that suited her just fine. She didn't need any complications in her life at the moment. Hannah more than filled any spare time she had. She turned over in the big double bed and pounded her pillow into shape with unnecessary vigour.

There had been the odd suitor since Matthew died, but none had remotely stirred her blood or her heart and she had never repeated any of the dates more than once. Perhaps she would never marry again, never find a man to replace Matthew? She shut her eyes and let her thoughts roam where they would.

She had known Matthew forever: they had grown up next door to each other from babies and she couldn't remember a time when she hadn't been going out with him. Marriage had been a natural progression. He was as familiar to her as her own skin, and life had been comfortable, peaceful and relaxed with him—no big highs, no desperate lows. Perfect. She curled into a little ball in the warmth of the bed. Their lovemaking had been gentle and infrequent, but that had suited both of them. They had been busy with their separate careers. She didn't believe in the sort of mindless passion one read about in books, anyway. She smiled whimsically in the darkness. Such emotion was a figment of writers' imaginations, poetic licence, and if it became a reality would probably prove to be unbearably uncomfortable.

The last three years had been a hard struggle, she reflected quietly, and painful at times, but she had managed to get through by her own determination and fortitude, finding within herself a tenacity she hadn't known she possessed. She had still been a child in many ways when Matthew died, protected and cocooned by circumstances and his love, but she had had to grow up very suddenly, and now her hard-won independence was precious, very precious.

She straightened in the bed, fingering her wedding-band as her thoughts wandered on. It hadn't occurred to her for a long time to take it off—in a way it was a solid link with Matthew that time couldn't erase—but when a friend had hinted she ought to think about doing that very thing, she had been shocked and horrified. Hannah deserved all her time and love for the next few years. Her daughter had been cruelly robbed of her natural father and no one, no one, could replace a father's love. She had seen too many situations where the children of a first marriage were subtly pushed aside as a new baby made an appearance. No. She wouldn't betray Matthew's memory or Hannah's trust by giving her anything less than her whole heart. Besides . . . She twisted restlessly in the bed. She had got used to being alone, to making her own decisions, *she had*. And everyone got lonely at times, even people who had been happily married for years.

No, everything was fine in her world, just fine. It didn't occur to her that this was the first time she had ever had to assure herself of the fact, which was probably just as well because sleep was a long time in coming. A certain hard, masculine face, with eyes the colour of a winter sky, kept getting annoyingly in the way.

CHAPTER TWO

LYDIA awoke very early the next morning, aware that she had been dreaming but unable to remember what about. But it had been a disturbing dream. She flicked her long blonde hair out of her eyes and glanced at the tiny alarm next to the bed. Five o'clock. Even Hannah wasn't stirring yet. She padded through to the small bedroom next to hers and stared down at the delicate baby face of her tiny daughter. She had been asleep when Lydia had got home the night before. She said a quick mental prayer for staunch grandmothers who insisted baby-sitting was a joy, but she had missed the night-time routine of bath and then story in bed with Hannah. She wished she could see more of Matthew in the minute features, but they were all her own. Everyone commented on the remarkable likeness between mother and daughter.

Within an hour, the instant Hannah opened huge, liquid brown eyes, in fact, the small house was a hive of activity, the normal morning routine of breakfast, shower and dressing taking all Lydia's concentration.

'You didn't kiss me night-night, Mummy.' Hannah's face was reproachful as she spooned cornflakes into her rosebud mouth. 'Gamma told the story all wrong.'

'Did she, darling?' Lydia stroked the top of the silky blonde head lovingly. 'You didn't tell her that, did you?'

'Course not.' Hannah was a true diplomat even at three. 'Are you going to pick me up from nursery today?'

'I doubt it, sweetheart.' Lydia knelt down by the breakfast stool and cupped the heart-shaped face in her hands. 'Did Grandma tell you about my job?'

'Uh-huh.' Hannah was distinctly disenchanted. 'But I want *you* to pick me up.'

'Well, this job is a bit different from my usual ones,' Lydia said carefully. 'The man I work for needs me to work much longer hours sometimes, but he is going to give me a lot of money if I do that. How about if we think of a new bedroom for you? You could choose the curtains and quilt and everything, even a new carpet if you want.'

'Really?' Hannah planted a swift milky kiss on her cheek. 'Can I have Pretty Pony, Mummy? Sophie has.' Sophie was her best friend at nursery and the two were inseparable most of the time.

'I should think so.' Lydia rose to look down at the small face smilingly. 'But you must promise to be good for Grandma when she picks you up and brings you home, even if I'm very late. I've only got the job for a little while, so we need to get as much money as we can for your room, don't we?'

'Yep.' Hannah obviously realised she was on to a good thing. 'Gamma says I'm her little angel,' she continued, fishing for praise which Lydia dutifully gave. 'Little angel' was pushing things a bit far, but then she had never wanted a placid child anyway.

She was in her office at just before nine after dropping Hannah off at the nursery, which unfortunately was in the opposite direction to the Strade office-block, and found Wolf was already at his desk, his black head bent over a long report as she tapped nervously at the interconnecting door. 'Come in, Lydia, don't stand on ceremony.' He didn't raise his head as he spoke and she wondered for an instant if he was telepathic as well. 'You can get straight on with that dictation from yesterday,' he said, after making a few notes in the margin before raising his head. 'I have an appointment at the other end of the city in an hour, so you should have a relatively undisturbed day.' He didn't smile.

The fine silk shirt he wore exactly matched the clear sapphire-blue of his eyes, she thought inconsequentially as she smiled and nodded her reply before leaving the room, and his aftershave—— She caught her thoughts abruptly, annoyed at the way they were heading. His aftershave was *aftershave*, that was all, she told herself sharply as she sat down at her desk and pulled out her notebook. He had probably paid a fortune to get the sort of reaction her senses had made when the sensual, intoxicatingly masculine fragrance had reached her nose.

She worked steadily for the next half-hour, pausing as he left to take a note of where he could be reached, her face bland and polite as he rapped out the telephone number and name of the firm, his face preoccupied and his voice remote.

There were several interruptions during the morning, but none she couldn't handle, and after snatching a quick meal in the canteen at lunchtime she continued to work her way through the pages of dictation until three, when a courteous knock at her outer door interrupted her as she had almost completed the notes.

'Come in.' The polite smile on her face widened as the tall, good-looking man who had poked his head round the door spoke her name in surprise.

'Lydia? What on earth are you doing here?'

'Mike!' She felt inordinately pleased to see a friendly face in the huge, overwhelmingly decorous establishment. 'How nice to see you. I'd completely forgotten you work here.'

'You're not working for Wolf, are you?' He came fully into the room and walked over to her desk, his eyes bright with interest. Mike Wilson was the husband of one of her oldest friends, Anna, who had been a tower of strength to her when Matthew died, often arriving un-announced when she was feeling at her lowest pitch to whisk her out to lunch and provide a rock-like shoulder to cry on. Lydia didn't know Mike that well—usually the two women met during the day when the agency didn't have any work for Lydia, or at the weekend when Mike was playing his endless rounds of golf—but whenever they had met, Mike had seemed warm and pleasant, if slightly effusive.

'Temping.' She smiled up at him ruefully. 'The agency dropped me in the deep end this time, straight to the top.'

'I rather think that's a contradiction in terms, but I know what you mean.' Mike grinned sympathetically. 'Bit of a slave-driver, isn't he, from what I've heard?'

'I don't know really, I've only been here a day or so.' A little alarm bell, deep in the recess of her mind, tolled warningly. There had been something in his face, she couldn't quite define what, that had made the words more than what they seemed at face value and, ridicu-lously, she felt a surge of defensive loyalty to Wolf without knowing why.

'Well, this is a nice surprise.' He wandered round the side of her desk as he spoke, glancing idly at the papers lying on the top of it as he smiled down at her. 'Wait till I tell Anna.'

'How is she? I haven't seen her for a couple of weeks,' Lydia said uncomfortably, feeling she should cover the detailed report on an important contract that she had just completed and printed, but knowing that it would look as though she suspected him of being nosy.

'Fine, fine. You know Anna, nothing gets her down.' He gestured towards the door of Wolf's office, still with his eyes on her desk. 'I presume the great man is elsewhere?'

'Yes.' To her relief he moved round the front of the desk again and bent down with his elbows resting on the wood as he spoke quietly.

'Well, that being the case, could I make a suggestion, Lydia? Wolf is a little . . . difficult about his personal secretary fraternising with the mere workers.' There it was again, that faint caustic note. 'The reputable Mrs Havers was a positive iceberg. Have you met her?' Lydia shook her head silently. 'Well, you haven't missed anything,' he continued with a faint grin. 'Anyway, it might be better for you if Wolf doesn't know we're old friends. He wouldn't like it, and as you'll only be around for a short time it seems silly to make waves, don't you think?'

'Well, I——'

'It might make things a bit uncomfortable for me too,' Mike continued quietly. 'You never know how Wolf is going to jump on things like this.'

'Well, of course I don't want to do anything that might reflect on you, Mike,' Lydia said quickly. 'It's just that it seems . . . unnecessary.'

'It isn't, believe me.' He smiled quietly. 'Well, do we have a deal, then?'

'Well, I can't see it matters one way or the other, so I suppose it's all right,' she said hesitantly.

'Good girl.' His smile widened. 'And how about you and that delightful little daughter of yours coming to

Sunday lunch soon? I haven't seen her in months. I'll get Anna to ring you, shall I?'

'That would be nice, thank you.' She forced a smile.

'And don't forget, not a word about our little secret.' He leant across and kissed her lightly as he had done several times in the past, a social gesture, nothing more.

'Good afternoon.'

If the ceiling had suddenly fallen in on her Lydia couldn't have reacted more violently. She shot out of her chair, hand to mouth, as she stared at Wolf's dark countenance in the doorway. It was clear he had heard, and seen, more than enough. 'I—I didn't know you were back,' she stammered, aware she had gone a brilliant red.

'Obviously.' He eyed Mike coldly. 'I presume you are in these offices for a reason, Mike?'

Mike had recovered far more quickly than she had, thrusting his hands casually in his pockets as he faced Wolf with an easy grin. 'Just wanted a word with you about the figures for Kingston,' he said calmly, 'if it's convenient?'

'Perhaps later.' Wolf's narrowed gaze brushed Lydia's hot face before he gestured to the finished work on her desk. 'Bring that in, would you? I'll glance through it before I do anything else. I want some of those letters to go off tonight.' His voice was infinitely cold, and she shivered as she glanced at Mike before gathering the files together. 'I'll ring you if I have time today, Mike.' It was a dismissal, and Mike went without another word, not even glancing in Lydia's direction as he left.

She followed Wolf into his office and placed the work on his desk. 'You've been busy.' He was looking at the pile of correspondence as he spoke, but she felt the words were the proverbial two-edged sword and remained silent. 'Sit down, Lydia.'

She sank into the chair facing his desk as he seated himself without taking his eyes off her troubled face. 'I didn't know you knew my financial director,' he said slowly, his voice expressionless but as cold as ice. 'You didn't mention it.'

She stared at him helplessly. What on earth was the matter with the man? Why did it matter to him who she knew anyway? 'I...' There was something so chilling in his face that it was freezing her thoughts. 'I didn't know I had to,' she said weakly, his aggressiveness making her feel twice as guilty as she did already.

'How long have you known him?'

This was ridiculous, she thought frantically. Pull yourself together, Lydia, explain you are a friend of Anna's, *talk* to the man. But she couldn't. Those ice-blue eyes were totally unnerving and, when she thought back to how the little tableau in the office must have seemed, embarrassment sent its red fingers all over her face. 'I don't know...' She tried desperately to think of how long Anna and Mike had been married. 'I think—— '

'No matter.' He straightened suddenly in his chair as though he had just come to a decision, and she stared at him, alarmed.

'Do you often wear your hair loose for the office?' he asked coldly as his gaze moved to the soft, silky locks lying in a shining veil across her shoulders.

'My hair?' She raised an unconscious hand to her head as she stared back at him. What had her hair to do with this?

'I prefer it tied back in the sort of style you wore yesterday,' he said coolly. 'As my secretary you have a certain reputation to maintain, and a neat, unassuming appearance gives the sort of impression I like in my staff. There are always men who are inclined to stand and waste time by the desk of a pretty woman, given the slightest encouragement.'

She really couldn't believe what she was hearing. She stared at him open-mouthed as she wondered if what she had heard was what he had really said. 'Exactly what are you saying?' she asked, after a moment of stunned silence.

'I'm saying that I would prefer a more discreet hair-style,' he said calmly as he picked up the phone that had begun to ring on his desk and gestured for her to leave. 'If you don't mind.'

There was nothing she could do but leave him to take the call, but as she returned to her own office her wits returned along with a flood of hot colour in her face. The cheek of it. The absolute cheek of it! Once that call ended she would tell him that she did mind, she minded very much, the arrogant, overbearing——

'Could I leave this with you for Mr Strade, please?' She came out of her silent fury to see one of the office juniors timidly holding out a large sealed envelope. 'It's from Mr Collins in Personnel.'

'Of course.' Lydia smiled at the nervous girl, who couldn't have been a day over sixteen, as she took a deep, silent breath. When that call ended, Wolf Strade, *when it ended* ... But half an hour later she was still waiting, by which time her anger had cooled, along with her face, and reason had asserted itself. This was a golden opportunity to get on her feet financially, and if she had to put up with this unpleasant, unreasonable male chauvinist pig as the cloud on which the silver lining was placed, then so be it.

But surely he didn't expect to choose her clothes and her hairstyle, did he? Even the reputable Mrs Havers couldn't have tolerated that, surely? She sat back in the chair with a puzzled little sigh. She didn't understand a thing about this man and, worse still, she didn't understand how he could get under her skin so badly. She had worked for more than a few awkward types in the last three years, but the most she had felt in the past was minor irritation accompanied occasionally by silent contempt for their crassness. But Wolf Strade... He was different. Totally different. And she had a good few months to get through yet. Could she do it? She frowned. Of course.

She thought of Hannah's bright little face as they had chatted about a Pretty Pony beanbag to match the rest of her proposed new bedroom, and sighed resignedly. But it wasn't going to be easy. She had the feeling Wolf Strade didn't like her much, even if he appreciated her attributes as a secretary. Still—she glared across at the closed door as a tiny flame of anger reignited—he shouldn't have given her the job, should he? She was blowed if she was going to be bullied into altering either her manner or her appearance to suit that pompous swine.

Nevertheless, the next morning she found herself fixing her long hair into a loose knot on the back of her head even as she told herself it was simply because it was less trouble that way. Wolf made no comment when she knocked and opened the door of his office to announce her arrival, wondering as she did so if he lived at the office. He was always around when she left at night and immersed in work when she arrived. She had been right. He *was* a machine.

'Could you work on these tapes before you do anything else?' he commanded abruptly as he handed her two audio-tapes from his desk. 'It's a report involving some complex financial data and I want it done immediately. And make sure you get the numbers right,' he added tersely.

'Of course, Mr Strade.' The tone and the name were a cold rebuke, and he raised his head abruptly to meet the dark, angry gleam in her eyes.

They stared at each other for a good thirty seconds before he surprised her utterly by leaning back in his chair and running his hand across his eyes with a weary gesture that spoke of utter exhaustion. 'I'm sorry, I sounded very rude.' The icy blue eyes were a little dazed, she realised suddenly, almost as though he hadn't slept. 'I've been here all night working on this damn mess. Why I employ an accounts department and do the work myself, I'll never know...'

'You've been here all night?' She saw the shirt was the same one he had worn the day before, but definitely the worse for wear, and the black stubble on his square chin made her heart give a solid little kick against her breasts before she could control it.

'Crazy, eh?' His smile was very boyish and rueful, and again her heart jerked uncomfortably. 'The graveyards are full of guys like me who can't let go of a problem until they've beaten it.'

'Or it beats them,' she added quietly.

'Yeah, maybe.' He settled back in the big black leather chair, stretching his hands above his head in a way that brought the muscled wall of his chest into stark prominence against the blue silk of his shirt. Some time during the night he had undone his tie and opened the first few buttons of his shirt, and now the sight of the dark, rough body-hair that covered his chest made her hands damp and her throat dry. What is the matter with me? she asked herself in disbelief. This wasn't sexual attraction, was it? She didn't fancy Wolf Strade of all people ... did she? 'How about a strong cup of coffee, and then maybe I'll grab a couple of hours' sleep on the couch before the meeting at eleven?'

'Weak tea would be better if you're going to sleep,' she answered automatically as her gaze flicked to the large studio couch in a shadowed corner of the huge room. She didn't want to be here when he lay down on that thing. She didn't even try to analyse why.

'I said coffee.' The cold authority was back in his voice but she didn't mind; that other Wolf was too dangerous to contemplate. 'And strong,' he added warningly.

'Coming up.'

Thankfully he was still sitting in the chair when she returned with the coffee a few minutes later, and she hurried out of the room after depositing the cup in front of him without speaking, her cheeks flushed.

At a quarter to eleven she was just contemplating gathering every scrap of courage she possessed and venturing into his office to wake him, when the connecting door opened and he stood framed in the doorway, blinking a little in the harsh artificial light overhead. 'If anyone arrives early, sit them down out here until I buzz,' he said abruptly, his eyes red-rimmed. 'I'm just going for a wash and brush-up.'

'Where?' she squeaked nervously, having visions of her room filled to overflowing with irate managers as they waited and waited.

'The washroom next door.' He glanced at her in surprise. 'Didn't you know it was there for your use too?

keep a change of clothes in there for emergencies—you can do the same if you wish.'

'I don't think that will be necessary,' she said stiffly, 'and how could I know it was there if you didn't see fit to tell me?'

'By using your initiative?'he suggested coolly.

'My initiative?' All thoughts of Hannah's bedroom faded into insignificance. 'In the three days since I've worked for you I haven't had time to breathe, let alone go exploring this block of concrete.' She glared at him angrily. 'It's got nothing at all to do with initiative, Mr Strade.'

'I thought blondes were supposed to be cool and un-emotional,' he said drily, studying her angry face with a superior frown. 'Are you like this with your husband?'

'Mr Strade, I——' She stopped abruptly as hot colour flooded her pale, creamy skin in a hectic flush. She couldn't ever remember having a cross word with Matthew. Life had been a flat, tranquil sea with him, with the days stretching out before them, calm and un-troubled. In fact, until she had met Wolf Strade, she could have sworn on oath that she had the mildest of tempers.

'And the name's Wolf.' His voice disappeared as he stepped through the doorway, and as she sank back in her seat she was aware of feeling slightly disloyal to Matthew's memory without understanding why. She stared at her wedding-ring for a long painful moment and then turned resolutely to the word processor and began to work. These fluttery feelings of excitement and agitation were a direct result of her nerves coping with the unusual sensations of anger and irritation, that was all. *That was all*. And in view of the self-opinionated, downright arbitrary despot she had been thrust into contact with, it wasn't surprising either. She had never met anyone, male or female, who could make her so mad so quickly by doing so little. He was so cold, so self-contained. Didn't *anything* touch him?

At five to eleven he reappeared in the doorway restored to his usual immaculate self, black hair slicked back, face shaven and a fresh grey silk shirt replacing the blue of the day before. He looked gorgeous. She held his glance with a cold composure that was the best piece of acting she had ever done, and listened as he gave her a list of files he needed for the meeting. As she deposited them on his desk two minutes later she caught a whiff of his aftershave and despised herself for the way her stomach clenched in an involuntary response, but she was honest enough to admit there wasn't a thing she could do about it. For some strange reason her body was determined to be aroused by a man she both disliked and disapproved of. Did he know? She glanced at his bent head as he checked through the files, and her heart thudded against her chest. She would die if he did. Just die.

'Right.' As he raised his head she saw his face was preoccupied and distant, the ice-blue eyes cold and hooded as they met hers. 'I'd like you to sit in on this one, Lydia, and take notes, OK?' She nodded quietly as a rush of relief made her light-headed. He didn't know, and she would have to make darn sure he never suspected even for a second if she wanted to keep her job. Thank goodness she had said she was married; it would probably never even cross his mind that she was attracted to him in a physical sense. 'Record anything Mike Wilson says, incidentally.' He paused, and the handsome, cruel face hardened into stone. 'No matter how obtuse.

OK?' He was watching her very closely and she felt a little shiver flicker down her spine.

'Why?' she asked carefully.

He shrugged slowly. 'You'll know soon enough, if my suspicions are right.' He lowered his head in dismissal.

At exactly eleven o'clock her office filled as though by magic, and as she ushered the group of men through she reflected, with wry uncomfortable humour, that Wolf had certainly got them well-trained. As the meeting progressed she didn't understand half of what she took down, but dutifully recorded everything in case she missed something vital.

It was a long day and an arduous one and, as she put the minutes of the meeting on Wolf's desk at just after six, she was conscious of an illogical, and quite unreasonable, sense of injustice that he should still appear cool and razor-sharp whereas she was visibly wilting.

'Your friend has been on the take.' It took a second for the words to register, spoken as they were in such a casual tone.

'Mike? No.' She raised shocked eyes to his. 'What are you going to do?' She somehow knew instantly it was true.

'It has already been done.' She looked away, her mouth unconsciously tightening at the flinty hardness in his face. 'You refuse any requests for references and refer any queries concerning him directly to me.'

'You've sacked him?' she asked with a horrified gasp.

'Too damn true.' He was flicking through the work she had just given him as he spoke, his head lowered. 'He'll be lucky if he gets a job sweeping the roads after I've finished with him.'

'But surely——?' She stopped abruptly as the ice-blu gaze switched to her face. This was awful, *awful*—poor Anna.

'Yes?' His tone was not encouraging.

'If it wasn't actually illegal…?' Her voice trailed away at the darkness in his face. 'I mean——'

'I know what you mean.' He shook his head tightly as he settled back in his chair, the razor-sharp eyes hard on her face. 'And, no, it wasn't "actually" illegal, not at this stage, but it would have been.' He eyed her grimly. 'You think I ought to have let the thing progress until I could throw a court case at him?'

'Of course not.' She flushed slightly at the hard scrutiny. 'But have you asked him why he did it?'

'I'm not interested in why,' he said coldly. 'He lied to me, that was his first big mistake, and then he thought an abject apology and a great deal of grovelling could extricate him from his foolishness. That was his second error of judgement.' He moved forward in the chair and lowered his gaze to the papers again. 'I won't tolerate being lied to, Lydia. I never have.'

'Oh.' She was glad he was looking downwards and missed the sudden surge of hot, guilty colour into her cheeks. 'Well, if there's nothing else, I'll say goodnight.'

'Wait a moment and I'll give you a lift home,' he said casually, still with his eyes on the papers in front of him. 'I'm dog-tired and enough is enough. The rest of this will wait.'

'There's no need.' She spoke so hastily that the words came out in a breathless rush. 'I don't want to take you out of your way and——'

'Get your coat.' It was as though she hadn't spoken.

'I…' She thought frantically for a cast-iron excuse to refuse the lift, but nothing came to mind, and as she stood hesitating in front of him he swept the papers into a neat pile and raised his head, his eyes blank.

'Well, go on,' he said irritably as he moved from the desk towards the coat-stand in the corner of the room. 'I haven't got all night.'

She hesitated for one more moment and then turned quickly and sped into the outer office, her thoughts in turmoil. She didn't want a lift with him, she *didn't*, she thought, panic-stricken as she slipped into her coat and checked the word processor was switched off. How was she going to make conversation with this iceberg of a man on the way home, and what if he expected to be asked in? He wouldn't, though, of course he wouldn't— would he...? She shut her eyes for a moment and prayed for calm. But if he did, she could say her husband was at work, or away, or something. Her eyes snapped open as he appeared in the doorway, his big black overcoat and heavy, dark briefcase adding to the image of formidable imperiousness.

Why had she started this? she asked herself desperately. Why had she lied? A tremor raced through her as she remembered his face when he had spoken of Mike Wilson's deceit. She should have come out in the open, made her position as a widow clear, and then the ball would have been in his court. And she hadn't explained properly about Mike either.

'Ready?' He waved a dismissive hand towards the door and followed her out into the corridor, his face remote and withdrawn and his body straight. She glanced at him carefully as the lift took them swiftly downwards. She knew why she had lied. It was there in the almost tangible signals of dissociation his body was sending to hers, the total repudiation of any involvement, however slight, on a personal level. He wanted an efficient ma-

chine in his office. That was all. If she had said she was
in effect single again . . . She nodded to herself mentally.
She had done the only thing possible in the circumstances. And of course he wouldn't want to come in
for coffee—one didn't fraternise with machines, after
all.

'You seem to be settling in very well.'

It was as she opened her mouth to reply to the obviously forced cool pleasantry that the lift shuddered to
a halt between floors, the momentary imbalance of the
big box shaking her off her feet and throwing her against
the solid bulk of his chest. His arms opened automatically to receive her as he in turn stumbled against the
wall of the lift, and for a breath-stopping moment she
was aware of being held in his arms, her face lifted up
to his, for all the world like two lovers about to kiss as
the lights flickered and dimmed.

'Are you all right?' Afterwards she realised he hadn't
reacted as she would have imagined by pushing her im-
patiently, or even distastefully, away. In fact his arms
tightened fractionally as he looked down into her
frightened upturned face, in which the darkness of her
eyes stood out like two velvet pools. 'Don't worry, lifts
have a habit of playing silly devils,' he reassured her
softly.

'Do they?' She tried to smile but the combination of
her fear of plunging to her death trapped in this little
metal box and, more especially, his closeness was making
her feel as helpless as a child. Although certainly her
body was reacting in a way that was definitely not child-
like, she countered wryly as she carefully eased herself
away from him. He was holding her loosely now, his
hands under her elbows, but the smell and feel of him

were all around her and they were...unsettling. And thrilling. Undeniably thrilling.

'You haven't hurt yourself?' For a split second she considered saying yes so that he would hold her a little longer, but that impulse alone was enough to shock her out of his hold as she shook her head, moving back a pace quickly.

What on earth's the matter with me? she asked herself weakly as he moved across the few feet of space and pressed the emergency button, his movements cool and controlled and his face expressionless. Is it sexual frustration? She shut her eyes briefly and prayed for the trembling that had taken over her limbs to still. But she didn't even have a sex drive, did she? Or not until three days ago, anyway.

'Claustrophobia.'

'What?' She opened startled eyes to see his face inches from her own again, and the next moment he had taken her into his arms, stroking her face comfortingly as he held her close against him.

'The panic you're feeling,' he said softly, his voice deep and low. He had seen her trembling and put it down to claustrophobia? She said a mental thank you to her guardian angel. 'It's perfectly natural and you'll be out of here in a few minutes. Just relax and let me take the load—you're doing fine.'

This wasn't helping, it definitely wasn't helping, she thought weakly as he enfolded her into him, wrapping his overcoat round her as he held her next to his heart. He thought she was scared to death but, instead of the biting scorn she would have expected, he was displaying a tenderness that was alarming. She was immensely glad a few seconds later when the emergency button buzzed loudly and the small intercom next to it crackled out security guard's voice. 'Hello? Is anyone in there?'

'Rogers?' Wolf moved across to answer and Lydia leant limply against the wall of the lift, her heart thudding as she watched him. 'My secretary and I are in here. What the hell's happening?'

'I'm sorry, Mr Strade,' the male voice answered promptly, 'but there's some sort of a power-cut that's affected all this side of the road. I understand it's being dealt with as quickly as possible, but I'm afraid there's nothing we can do at the moment.'

'Brilliant.' He glanced across at her quickly before speaking again. 'Any idea how long before we're out?'

'Not long, sir.' There was a brief pause while they heard him talking to someone else. 'About twenty minutes or so at the most.'

'Right, keep me informed.'

As he turned to face her fully again she spoke quickly in case he thought he had to continue the role of comforter. 'I'm fine now, really.' She smiled brightly. 'It was just the suddenness of it all.'

'Good.' He clearly thought she was just trying to be brave, because the expression of gentle concern that was so surprising on the harsh features didn't lessen. 'Well, we may as well make ourselves comfortable while we wait. I suggest you take off your coat—it's already getting a little warm in here.'

'Right.' As she shrugged the jacket off her shoulders he moved quickly and drew it down her arms, his light touch burning her flesh as his fingers briefly made contact.

'Sit on this.' He made his own coat into a large cushion, crouching down as he plumped it into shape. As she sat down on the wad of material he gestured at

e. 'Do you mind?' he asked mildly. 'I don't like
se things at the best of times.'

'Of course not.' He stood up again, for which she was
supremely grateful. The way the material of his trousers
had moulded to his thighs had caused her breathing a
few problems. He unbuttoned his jacket, revealing the
grey silk shirt tucked into the flat waistband of his
trousers, and then loosened his tie, undoing the first few
buttons of his shirt. Somehow, in the close confines of
the small lift, the action was painfully intimate, but for
the life of her she couldn't draw her eyes away from his
broad shoulders and muscled chest, the dark body-hair
beneath the shirt causing hot colour to surge into her
cheeks. Was he hairy all over? She shut her eyes against
the thought.

'OK?' Her eyes snapped open to see him sitting against
the opposite wall, his narrowed gaze fixed on her face.
'You look hot.'

'No, I'm absolutely fine.' She smiled brightly.

As she brushed a wisp of hair from her cheek his eyes
followed the action, his gaze resting on the smooth
blondeness of her hair. 'How did you come to get such
unusual colouring?' he asked suddenly. 'Your hair is so
fair and yet your eyes are almost black.'

'I don't know.' She tried for a casual smile—that
piercing gaze was more than a little unnerving. 'Some
errant gene, I suppose, but it must be a strong one.
Hannah, my daughter, is exactly the same. Everyone says
she is a carbon copy of me.'

'Do they?' There was something in his expression she
couldn't read and it unnerved her still more. 'Your
husband is a very lucky man to have two beautiful
females to love,' he said, after a few strangely tense seconds had ticked by.

Lydia's stomach clenched and she looked away quickly, her eyes downcast. How could she reply to that? She took a long, hidden breath and prayed for calm. 'How long have we been in here now?' she asked tensely.

'About ten minutes.' He didn't glance at his watch as he spoke; his gaze never left her face. 'Shut your eyes a moment and try to relax,' he added gently. 'Take a few deep breaths and regulate your breathing.' He thought there was a danger of her hyperventilating? Lydia thought weakly. How right he was, but not for the reason he imagined! Nevertheless, she did as he instructed, leaning back against the wall of the lift and shutting her eyes tight as she folded her arms protectively over her breasts. The dim light from the emergency batteries in the lift's back-up system produced a dull charcoal glow against her closed eyelids, and after a few seconds she heard Wolf's briefcase snap open and the rustle of papers.

He was going to work *now*? She opened incredulous eyes to see him crouched over a long report, a slight frown wrinkling his brow as he peered at the small figures in the shadowy gloom. He was unbelievable, quite unbelievable. Didn't he ever stop working? She smiled bemusedly.

'What?' She hadn't been aware that the blue eyes had flicked upwards, but now saw they were trained on her face.

'I'm sorry?' She was flustered and it showed.

'You were smiling, a Mona Lisa smile if I may say so,' he added softly. 'Why?'

'Oh, nothing, it was just——' She stopped abruptly as she wondered if she dared tell him. Oh, blow it, he *had* asked, after all. 'I was wondering if you ever stop working,' she said quietly, 'that's all.'

'Do I detect a note of disapproval?' he asked smoothly as he crouched back on his heels, the position emphasising strong muscled legs and hard inner thighs.

'Not really.' She smiled with what she hoped came across as cool composure. 'I'm sure it needs your sort of dedication to stay at the top in this business——'

'You're right,' he interrupted expressionlessly, 'it does.' He stood up slowly, leaning back against the wall with his arms crossed and his eyes narrowed as he looked down at her. 'But that is only part of it. I like what I do, that's the bottom line.'

'Yes...' She shook her head slowly. 'But incidents like the Mike Wilson thing, don't they bother you at all?'

'Mike Wilson has been dealt with before he could do any damage,' he said coldly, 'and, more importantly, has been *seen* to be dealt with. He will serve as a timely example of what happens if anyone is stupid enough to try and cross me, so, if anything, I have gained, not lost, from the episode. That being the case, why should it bother me?'

She stared at him silently, shocked by the blatant ruthlessness his words revealed. 'But he has a wife and child,' she murmured, after a pregnant pause. 'You said yourself he'll never get another job——'

'That is his concern, not mine.' The handsome face was stony now. 'He had an excellent and extremely well-paid position with me, which he chose to put in jeopardy through his own greed. He has lived an executive life-style for several years, complete with large house, private schooling for his boy, all the trappings wealth brings, and that has been on the salary I have paid him. If you are asking me to feel guilty, forget it. I don't.' He eyed her grimly. 'Besides which, the Mike Wilsons of this world always get by,' he finished brusquely.

He was right. She had to admit there was more than a grain of truth in what he said, and he had had the option of giving Mike enough rope to hang himself but decided against it, and yet... She too rose, very slowly, to stand looking at him across the few feet of space. Did he have to be so cold, so remote, so untouched by it all? She doubted if he had any normal feelings at all or, if there were a few, they were deeply encased in solid ice. 'I can understand what you are saying but——' She stopped abruptly, not quite knowing how to continue. This was her boss, when all was said and done, her bread and butter, so to speak.

'But?' His expression was cynical and cold, and suddenly Lydia knew he was totally aware of her feelings about the matter and they didn't bother him an iota. He was a man who would always do exactly what *he* thought was right in any situation in which he found himself, and to hell with the rest of the world. Her own mouth hardened, but even as she opened it to speak the security guard's voice crackled over the intercom again.

'Mr Strade?'

'Yes?' Wolf's voice was clipped.

'Any minute now, sir. Are you all right in there?'

'Fine, Rogers.' He bent, stuffing the papers back in his briefcase and gesturing to her coat by her feet. 'I suggest you put that back on,' he said calmly as he reached across for his own. 'No doubt it'll strike cold once we're out of this sauna.'

At the same moment that the lights flooded back on the lift began to move, but in the same instant it jerked violently, throwing Lydia off her feet for the second time that night as it stopped again. And this time she *was* frightened, petrifyingly so. 'Wolf?' He had caught her as she fell, the momentum of her body and the bending position he had been in sending him to his knees and now she lay across his lap, her face uplifted and hair fanning out across his arm as the knot came loose. There was one split second, as she looked up into the hard, masculine face above her own, when she knew what was about to happen and felt the blood pound through her veins, her body beginning to quiver in anticipation. His eyes were bright and glittering as they stared down into the velvet brown depths of hers, the desire she could read so plainly in his dark face hot and hard and incredibly sensual.

He was going to kiss her. The thought exploded into her mind, and now little tremors of helpless excitement reached her toes and curled the small pads into the soles of her feet as she envisaged his mouth on hers. She could feel his heart pounding against the solid wall of his chest and the expensive, heady, totally masculine smell of him pervaded every nerve and tissue.

She wanted him to kiss her. She wanted it more than she had ever wanted anything in her life and, strangely, the thought didn't seem shocking as his arms tightened and his eyes narrowed into brilliant blue slits.

Wolf. She was never sure even afterwards if she said his name out loud or just breathed it in her soul as a silent, helpless plea, but just as she thought his dark head would lower to hers, that she would know what it was like to be kissed by this fierce, powerful, cold man, he moved her from him, his face stiffening with unconcealed disgust and his body rigid with control.

CHAPTER THREE

As THE intercom coughed and spluttered, the sound seemed to explode into the deathly quiet of the tiny box and then Rogers's gruff voice spoke, his tone concerned. 'I'm sorry, Mr Strade, there seems to have been a minor hiccup. The circuit-breakers have tripped out due to their normal mode being broken, but it won't take me above five minutes to re-set them. Are you and the lady all right, sir?'

'Just get on with it, Rogers.' The security guard's voice had acted like a deluge of cold water, and immediately he had spoken, bringing the outside world into their small domain, an icy blankness had wiped all expression from Wolf's face. He helped her to her feet without speaking, his body stiff.

'Lydia?' She raised her hot face slowly, unable to take a verbal slap in the face after the contempt and scorn he had just shown so plainly, but she wouldn't blame him if he told her exactly what he thought. How could she have encouraged him like that? How could she? What on earth must he be thinking? She was supposed to be a married woman, after all, and she had practically begged—— 'It won't be long and we'll be out of here, OK?'

'Yes.' Her voice was small and bewildered and the sound of it made the harsh, masculine face in front of her tighten savagely, the hard features setting into stone. She had lain there and asked him to make love to her. Her mind shouted the accusation at her. And he had

47

anted to—well, what man wouldn't if it was offered so outrageously?

But he had had the moral strength to turn away, his disgust at her wantonness evident in every line of that handsome face. She couldn't bear this humiliation, she couldn't. The thoughts raced frantically through her mind as she tried desperately to pull herself together, fighting for the control that had seen her through so many difficulties and traumas in the last few years.

'I...' Her voice faltered and she took a deep breath before trying again. She had to retrieve this situation, dredge up some dignity from somewhere. 'I feel much better now, thank you, it was the panic...'

'Panic?' He looked at her blankly for a moment and then nodded slowly, his mouth tightening still more. 'You were scared to death, I know that, but I just want to say——'

'How long will it be before we are out?' She had seen his devastating brand of honesty once or twice in the three days she had worked for him, but she wished with all her heart he could let it slip just once. She couldn't talk about what had so nearly happened now, and if he tried to take the blame through perverse male pride it would make things ten times worse. A post-mortem at this moment was more than she could take.

He stared at her for a long, silent moment, the narrowed cold eyes tight on her face, and then took the cue she had given him with a cool equanimity that made her tangled thoughts seem even more confused. 'A couple of minutes more, no longer.'

She nodded weakly. Suddenly her safe, ordered little world had turned upside-down and she was stunned with the unexpectedness of it. The two or three minutes it took for the lift to resume its downward journey seemed like two or three hours, and for the whole time her heart was thudding against her breasts so hard it hurt. Not a word was spoken but the silence was deafening, banging against her ear-drums until she felt like screaming.

But nothing had *actually* happened. She forced herself to think logically, to apply reason to the shame and embarrassment. But he had known. He had known she wanted him to kiss her. What should she do? She glanced across at Wolf's stony face as he stood leaning against the far side of the lift, his eyes half closed and his body seemingly relaxed.

This time the lift started smoothly, gliding down to the ground floor and opening its doors with silky obedience. As she followed Wolf out to his Mercedes in its reserved spot just outside the main entrance, she contemplated, for a crazy moment, telling him the truth, but as he opened the passenger door of his car for her to enter one look at his dark face convinced her she didn't have the nerve. It might persuade him that he hadn't got a potential adulteress in his office, but if he knew she had deliberately misled him, secured the job on a whopper of a lie ... And he hadn't liked her defence of Mike; that was most certainly another nail in her coffin. She swallowed painfully.

'Your address?' His tone was clipped and short, and after she had given it she slid into the beautiful Mercedes and sat huddled tensely in the seat as he joined her, his face cold.

'Could you try and relax a little?' They had been travelling in silence for some minutes and she started violently as his voice, abrupt and deep, sounded at her side. 'I'm beginning to feel like some sort of pervert with you sitting halfway up the window like that.'

'What?' As she glanced at the large area of vacant space on the right-hand side of her seat, she realised she was indeed perched against the side of the car in a manner that he could well term insulting, and she slid quickly into the middle of the seat, her face flaming. Great. Now he'd think she was a split personality too! One minute a shameless temptress and the next the original shrinking violet. 'I'm sorry, I didn't realise.'

'I'm not sure if that makes it worse or better,' he said drily, with one swift, piercing glance at her red face. 'Look, I don't want anything to spoil our working relationship, Lydia——'

'It won't.' The reply was immediate as she cut off his voice. She couldn't talk about it, she just couldn't. Somehow the whole incident had opened up another side to him that had her tingling all over and, although the feeling wasn't unpleasant, in the circumstances it *was* intensely humiliating. He had rejected her with apparently the minimum of effort and that cool, devastatingly clear mind wasn't in the least affected. But she—she closed her eyes against her own weakness—she was aware of every tiny movement he made, of his strong, capable hands on the steering-wheel, his long, lean legs and powerful thighs...

'Good.' She felt his glance on her face again but didn't look at him.

'You turn right here.' She was unutterably thankful this nightmare journey would end soon. 'Then left at the corner.' He followed her instructions without speaking again, and when they drew up outside her house some minutes later she realised her hands were clenched together so tightly her fingers were numb.

'Thank you for the lift——' she began primly, fumbling for her handbag at her feet, but he had already opened his door, moving round the car and helping her out with an old-fashioned courtesy that was all the more seductively attractive for being entirely natural. 'Thank you——' she began again, only to be interrupted a second time as Hannah's bright little voice called to her from the top step seconds before her tiny daughter bounded across the three or four feet of paved front garden and into her arms. 'Mummeeee!' Hannah's voice was ecstatic. 'Mrs Thomson next door says I can have one of her kittens for my very own. Can I, Mummy? Can I?'

'This is Hannah.' She looked at Wolf warily over her daughter's head and surprised a look in his eyes that she couldn't quite fathom. Pain? Distress? Bitterness? Dislike? But then a shutter slid into place and the remote, cool gaze was the one she knew. 'Hannah, this is Mr Strade.'

'How do you do, Hannah?' he asked gravely, a smile touching the hard features briefly.

'Lo.' Hannah smiled back as she twisted round in Lydia's arms for a better view. 'My mummy works for you, doesn't she?'

'Indeed she does.' He moved towards the car as he spoke, clearly not wishing to prolong the moment, for which Lydia was extremely thankful. The weight of her lie had suddenly become like a noose round her neck.

'Do you like kittens?' Hannah was speaking directly to Wolf, who paused with his hand on the car door. 'They're little cats,' she added helpfully.

'Hannah, Mr Strade has got to go,' Lydia said hastily as her mother appeared in the lighted doorway to the house. This was fast becoming too much.

'Yes, I like kittens.' He looked at Hannah as Lydia held her close, their two heads touching as Hannah snuggled down in her mother's arms, and then raised a casual hand to the figure in the doorway before sliding into the interior of the car and starting the engine in the same movement.

'I like him.' As the car moved smoothly away Hannah waved vigorously, but the dark figure in the driving seat didn't respond. 'He's nice.'

'How do you know?' Lydia's mother asked smilingly as she joined them in the street, sharing a glance of amusement with Lydia over Hannah's head as they watched the tail-lights of the car disappear. 'You've only said hello to him.'

'He likes kittens.' That, as far as Hannah was concerned, was the end of the matter. 'And Mummy likes him, don't you, Mummy?'

Lydia smiled weakly. 'What's all this about Mrs Thomson and a kitten?' The diversion worked, but later that night, as she lay in bed with sleep a million miles away, Hannah's words came back to haunt her. *Did* she like him? She pictured the hard, handsome face and powerfully masculine body and a little shiver trickled down her spine, sensitising a hundred nerve-ends she had never known she had. 'Like' was not a word that applied to Wolf Strade somehow. One 'liked' neighbours or friends or the family doctor, but Wolf... She twisted in the big bed irritably. What on earth was she thinking about him for, anyway? He was her boss, that was all, a multimillionaire whose lifestyle was so at variance with hers they could have been on different planets. But he had wanted her... The thought was there before she could stop it and she sat up in bed jerkily, her face stricken.

'Oh, no, none of that, Lydia.' Her voice as she spoke into the dark room was tightly emphatic. 'You work for him, that's all, and the only reason he took you on in the first place was because he thought you were married and immune from any fancy ideas. Women chase him all the time, you *know* that, for goodness' sake.' But he *had* wanted her, the voice in her mind taunted quietly. She had read it in his eyes. It wouldn't mean a thing to a man like him, she answered silently, not a thing. In spite of the desire that had flared between them so swiftly, the wild hunger she had seen in his face, he had been able to push her aside without a qualm, although he must have sensed her surrender. Sensed it and shown his disgust at it too, the inexorable voice reminded her relentlessly. She groaned softly, the sound a little lost whimper in the emptiness of the silent room.

The next day was a Friday, and painful in the extreme as Lydia struggled to maintain a cool, efficient image while shrivelling up inside every time she glanced at Wolf's dark countenance, but after a normal family weekend Monday was easier and Tuesday more so. Wolf was his normal arrogant cold self, his blue eyes cool and remote if they caught hers, and gradually the incident in the lift became a little less stark as day followed hectic day. Once or twice she thought she caught him staring at her with an odd expression in the darkly lashed blue eyes, but his manner would change so swiftly when he caught her gaze that she told herself she was imagining things. And she *had* noticed he went to great pains not to touch her, even in the most abstract way, but then, he wasn't a physical man, she told herself uneasily...was he? Matthew hadn't been. She shook her head mentally at her naïveté where men were concerned, but then she had only ever known Matthew. The normal scenario of boy meets girl, the inevitable experimentation of life and love, had completely passed her by.

And she knew absolutely nothing about Wolf. This fact was brought home forcibly on the day Hannah was to collect the kitten from Mrs Thomson, it now having reached the requisite age of eight weeks. She had arranged to leave an hour early in order to pick Hannah up herself from nursery, and was just finishing the final pages of a complex financial report when a cursory knock at her outer door interrupted her train of thought.

'Yes?' The door had opened even as she spoke and a heavy gust of expensive perfume drew her head upwards.

'Is he in?' The woman who had just sauntered into the room was tall, willowy and so beautiful that Lydia found herself gaping for a startled second before she collected herself.

'Yes...' She reached for the buzzer on her desk. 'Who shall I say——?'

'Don't bother with that thing.' The throaty, attractive voice was warm and confident and wide blue eyes gave her the once-over a moment before the woman opened the door to Wolf's office and stepped through.

'But you can't——' Lydia followed through the open door a second later, her face aghast, to find the woman leaning over Wolf's desk to deposit a fleeting kiss on his mouth before turning to survey her in the doorway.

'It's OK, Lydia.' Wolf didn't look particularly pleased at the intrusion, but neither was he displaying the sort of anger she had expected.

'I'm sorry——'

'Oh, Wolf is used to my barging in at any time of the night or day, aren't you, darling...?' A perfect little rotund bottom seated itself on the corner of his desk, the manoeuvre exposing a great deal of slim, tanned leg as smiling blue eyes wandered over Lydia in open appraisal. 'He's my mentor. Is that the appropriate word, darling?'

'That's enough, Elda.' Wolf smiled back at the beautiful brunette indulgently. 'And get off my damn desk.'

The brunette's thin but beautifully shaped mouth pouted in a little grimace as she did as she was told, her movements elegant and unhurried. Where did she get such amazing self-assurance? Lydia wondered as she turned to leave. But then perhaps it wasn't surprising really. Sleek dark hair cut in an expert feathery style to complement the graceful head and long neck, huge blue eyes and a perfect skin added up to an impressive whole, and her clothes weren't from the local high street either!

As she returned to her desk, shutting the door quietly and firmly behind her, she found to her dismay that she was shaking slightly. She sat down with a little plop and took a long deep breath, willing her heart to calm down. So he had a girlfriend? So what? Of course a man like him wouldn't be short of female company, she knew that, didn't she?

But what a girlfriend! The thought was painful. And it wasn't exactly that he had a girlfriend that was bothering her, but the way he had looked at Elda. She hadn't seen that gentle, soft look on his face before and it had hurt her. Why, she didn't know.

Their working routine had settled down into a pattern that, despite the odd panic here and there, was relatively straightforward, although she certainly couldn't have called Wolf Strade an easy man to work for. He was blunt to the point of rudeness on occasion but, she had to admit, the social standing of the recipient didn't affect his brusqueness at all. He was simply a man who suffered fools badly, be they kings or paupers.

The buzzer on her desk interrupted her train of thought. 'Lydia? Could you arrange some coffee, please?' Wolf asked pleasantly.

'Certainly.'

She normally phoned down such requests but today she took the lift to the canteen herself. Somehow she didn't want to be in the office and, as she carried the tray in to Wolf ten minutes later, she knew why. There was something too cosy in his acceptance of Elda's easy intrusion.

'Cut along now, Lydia, and I hope all goes well with the kitten.' As Wolf gave one of his rare smiles Lydia saw Elda's blue eyes narrow in sudden sharp scrutiny.

'I'll just finish the last page of that report first.' She smiled with what she hoped was cool composure, nodded to Elda, who had now seated herself in the large easy chair opposite Wolf's desk, and walked quietly from the room, more shaken than she cared to admit. It was nothing to her who he saw in his private life, she told herself fiercely as she finished the report to the sound of occasional laughter from the connecting room, nothing at all.

Did he make long, passionate love to Elda? She didn't know where the thought came from, but it was enough to jerk her out of her seat as though she had been pricked with a pin. Of course he would, she answered herself irritably as she slipped into her jacket, her eyes stormy and her mouth unconsciously tight. A man like him didn't get to thirty-eight and remain single without perfecting his technique. And it would be *some* technique! She shut her eyes briefly and then resolutely turned her mind away from the dangerous path it was following. She was as bad as her predecessors. What had he called them? Oh, yes, empty-headed little bimbos. The chauvinistic phrase still had the power to make her mad. And *that* was the sort of man he was; she'd better remember it. He'd made it perfectly clear over the last few weeks that he viewed her in the same way as the office furniture, and it suited her just fine, *just fine*. Involvement with him, with any man, just wasn't on the cards.

'That's some frown.'

'What?' She hadn't heard him come into the room, but now she saw the connecting door was closed as he stood just in front of it, his eyes quizzical and his mouth straight.

'Is something wrong?' He leant against the door-jamb as he spoke, crossing his arms as he viewed her through narrowed eyes. 'You seem ... disturbed.'

'Disturbed?' She was acutely aware of Elda in the next room and the sudden desire to hit him hard was as shocking as it was irrational.

'Lydia ...' He paused as though he found it difficult to continue, but his voice was quite expressionless when he spoke. 'Is everything all right at home? I mean, are there any domestic difficulties that are worrying you, any problems?'

'Of course there aren't.' Her relief at his misinterpretation of her agitation was overwhelming. 'Everything's fine.' She dropped her eyes for a moment, her face flushing.

'Yes, it would be.' He stared at her for a long moment with expressionless eyes. 'He wouldn't be such a fool——' He stopped abruptly and moved to her desk, picking up the report she had finished. 'Goodnight, Lydia.' His voice was cold and abrupt and she stared at him for a moment, nonplussed by his coolness.

What had she done now? He turned and re-entered his office without looking at her again, a small muscle jumping in his jaw that convinced her she was right. She had done something to annoy him, but what? Suddenly she had the crazy impulse to fling open his door, march up to his desk and demand an explanation, but then a soft husky giggle from the inner room swamped her with cold reason. What was she thinking of, for goodness' sake? He hadn't said or done anything wrong, in fact he had shown concern, albeit frostily, that something was bothering her. And there was. She frowned helplessly at the shut door. But she couldn't put a name to it. All she knew was that from that moment in the lift she just couldn't view him in quite the same light. The incident had revealed a wildly passionate, sensual side to him that didn't fit in with the cold, intimidatingly intelligent individual of office hours and she wanted—— She cut her thoughts abruptly. She didn't know *what* she wanted! Yes, she did—the safe, comfortable, ordinary existence she had always known without disturbing night-time dreams that made her feel shamefully wanton if she recalled even a part of them.

She rubbed her hand across her hot face and took a deep breath as she buttoned her jacket and checked the word processor was switched off. She should never have worked for him in the first place, never have got embroiled in the lie that had seemed to stretch and grow in the last few weeks. Wolf never referred directly to her private life but there had been one or two instances when a negative reaction, a reiteration of her husband's place in her life, more by what she had not said than what she had, had proved itself necessary.

Hannah was thrilled with the kitten, a tiny scrap of fur and eyes that she immediately named Tiger because of its markings, and Lydia let her stay up later than usual after tea, watching them both through the open kitchen door as she made up a little basket for the animal and arranged a litter-tray in an alcove near the back door. She had just ventured up the somewhat rickety step-ladder to reach a small dish on top of one of the kitchen cupboards that was just right for such a tiny scrap when the phone rang, making her jump. Whether she leant over too far or the step-ladder slipped she was never quite sure, but the next moment she was clutching frantically at thin air as she fell, landing with a bone-jarring thud on the kitchen floor as the step-ladder caught her a stunning blow across the head as it collapsed at her side.

'Mummy! Mummy!' Hannah's voice was shrill with panic as she ran into the kitchen, the kitten disappearing under a chair, its back arched in fright.

'It's all right, Hannah.' She wanted to be sick, desperately, but she fought it along with the rising tide of blackness that was threatening to take her over. She couldn't pass out, not when Hannah was alone like this. 'Answer the phone quickly, darling,' she mumbled through numb lips, 'it's probably Grandma. Tell her I've fallen down and need some help.'

'Oh, Mummy...' As large tears welled up in Hannah's big brown eyes, Lydia used all her strength to speak again.

'Answer the phone, Hannah, quickly.' It was their lifeline. '*Now*, darling.' And then the rushing in her ears became like an express train and darkness closed in, shutting out Hannah's sobs and her own frantic desperation.

She could only have lost consciousness for a few minutes, and as she struggled back out of the roaring blackness her first thought was for Hannah. She must have spoken her daughter's name because a little voice answered immediately by her side. 'Yes, Mummy?'

'Don't worry, darling.' As her eyes focused on the small face she lay for a few seconds, willing the faintness away, and then moved gingerly, pulling herself into a sitting position with her back against the line of cupboards. 'I'm all right, Hannah, I promise.' Hannah nodded tearfully but looked far from convinced, and as Lydia opened her arms dived into them like a tiny, frightened rabbit. 'Did you answer the phone?' Lydia asked weakly, relaxing again as the little head nodded an affirmative. Thank goodness. Help was on the way.

As she sat with Hannah in her arms she tested each part of her body slowly and was relieved to find nothing seemed to be broken, although everything was hurting. How could she have been so stupid? She shut her eyes helplessly. She was usually so careful, so cautious.

After a few minutes Tiger's striped head peered warily round the kitchen door, only to disappear abruptly again as the front doorbell rang stridently. 'That will be Grandma.' Why hadn't her mother used her key? she thought wearily as she struggled painfully to her feet, Hannah trotting along by her side like a scared puppy.

She could feel each step in her head as she walked slowly to the door, and the short journey took all her concentration. She hadn't been aware her head had bled, but just as she reached the door she saw her white blouse was smudged with red, and as she raised her hand to her brow it came away sticky. Great, just great. If her mother hadn't panicked already she would throw a blue fit at the sight of blood. But it wasn't her mother who faced her as she opened the door.

'What the hell...?'

The shock of seeing Wolf on her doorstep was almost too much, and as she swayed he caught her arm firmly before bending slightly and whisking her up into his arms. It was only a step through the minute hall into the small but cosy lounge, and the open door at the far end which led into the kitchen was wide open, the step-ladder bearing evidence of the accident. 'I'm all right, really...' she murmured faintly as he deposited her with startling gentleness into the depths of the sofa.

The expression on his face told her how stupid her words had sounded in the circumstances, and he knelt down at her side before turning to speak to Hannah who was standing just behind them, her eyes wide and her face tear-smudged. 'Are you OK, sweet-pea?' She had never heard him speak in that tender tone of voice before and it did something to her heart that was almost painful. As Hannah nodded uncertainly he reached out an arm and drew the small child close, hugging her reassuringly before speaking again. 'Your mummy is going to be fine. She's just bumped her head a little, like you bump your knees if you fall over. Understand?' The small nod carried more assurance this time.

'That *is* all you've done?' He turned back to Lydia suddenly. 'No broken bones, no sprains?'

'I don't think so.' She tried to smile but the effort was too much. 'I've just got this awful headache.'

'How awful?' he asked grimly as his gaze took in her cloudy eyes and trembling mouth. 'Did you pass out?'

She nodded, but the action caused such excruciating pain that she gasped out loud, the whiteness of her face standing out in stark contrast to the blood on her forehead.

'Where's your husband? Matthew, isn't it?'

As Hannah opened her mouth Lydia jumped in first, her voice high with strain. 'Hannah, go and get ready for bed, darling. Just pop into your nightie, we'll have a wash in the morning.' The kitten made a cautious reappearance as she spoke, its bright green eyes enormous in the delicate face. 'I'll bring Tiger in to stay goodnight when you're in bed.' That did the trick, and as Hannah's feet disappeared up the stairs Wolf stood up slowly, his eyes concerned as he quietly glanced round the room.

'What's going on, Lydia?' She stared up at him, quite unable to speak. 'He's not living here, is he?' It was a statement rather than a question, and with the sick pounding in her head a lowering of her eyes was all she could manage. She ought to explain, she told herself weakly, now was the perfect opportunity and he wouldn't be too mad, would he? Not with her like this? But somehow, as he stood in front of her, his face uncharacteristically gentle and his eyes warm, she couldn't bring herself to speak, to see his expression change from one of tender concern to hard condemnation of her deceit. 'I thought something was wrong for the last week or two,' he said almost to himself. 'I should have guessed, especially with the kitten. That was to take Hannah's mind off it?' She stared at him, frozen in mind and body as she realised he thought Matthew had just recently left her. She couldn't let this continue, it was too awful, but as she opened her mouth to explain he knelt at her side again, his face rueful. 'Hell, there couldn't be a worse time for twenty questions, could there? Just relax, Lydia, I'm going to phone a doctor to check out that bump on your head——'

'No!' She caught hold of his arm. 'I'm OK, really, I don't want any fuss. Please, Wolf——'

'Lydia, you are going to see a doctor.' His eyes lingered on the gash on her forehead again. 'It's just a surface wound, but you may have concussion——'

'My mother will be here shortly and she'll stay the night.' She was gabbling, but she had to get him out of here before her mother arrived or Hannah came back and said something that would betray her.

'She knows?' he asked quietly, indicating her head.

'She phoned just as it happened. Hannah told her.'

'I think that was me.' He stared at her with brooding eyes. 'I was ringing to ask if you could come in a few minutes early to do a short prefix on that report. When Hannah answered the phone and said you'd fallen and needed help, I came straight here. Fortunately I hadn't left the office, so I was on the doorstep, so to speak.' He leant forward and stroked a strand of hair off her face as he spoke, his flesh warm and firm. She felt the contact in every nerve of her body.

'You were very quick,' she managed faintly.

'Tell me about it.' He smiled a crooked smile that would have made her weak at the knees if she wasn't already. 'Fortunately I didn't meet a police car on the way.'

Was this the icy, distant individual she knew? she asked herself unbelievingly. The aloof, cold tycoon who had everyone jumping through hoops at the office, including her?

'Now, first things first.' He eyed her consideringly as he stood up, shrugging his big black overcoat off his shoulders and slinging it on a nearby chair as he strode into her small, gleaming kitchen and lifted the step-ladder off the floor. 'I'm going to clean you up a bit and then ring my own doctor——' As she made an exclamation of protest he raised an authoritative hand. 'He's an old friend too and won't mind taking a look at you as a personal favour. Then, if we need to contact your mother, we will, otherwise...' He glanced across at her as he filled a basin with warm water as though he administered first aid to concussed secretaries every day. 'You can ring her in the morning,' he finished quietly. 'I guess she has been pretty upset by...what's happened, too?' The brief pause made her blush scarlet. She had to say something, she had to, even if he was furious——

'Mummeee.' Hannah's voice was a plaintive wail, and as Lydia made to rise Wolf gestured her back on the sofa sharply. 'Lie there and don't move,' he said firmly. 'Where's the damn cat?' As he whisked Tiger up in the palm of one hand Lydia struggled into a sitting position despite his ferocious glare.

'I need to say goodnight to her, reassure her.' She gulped deep in her throat as the room waved and spun. 'Please, Wolf, she'll be awake all night——'

'I'll carry you and the moggy, then.' He plonked Tiger in her arms and, as before, picked her up as though she weighed no more than a feather. It was a bit of a struggle up the narrow stairs, but she was oblivious to his careful manoeuvring. She could feel his heart beating steadily through his shirt, his jacket having been discarded along with his coat, could feel his arms strong and hard as they cradled her to him, see his dark face inches from her own and the smell of him... It was all around her, making her dizzy with an intoxicating delight that was more dangerous than any concussion.

I don't believe this is happening, she thought helplessly as he carried her into Hannah's small bedroom, depositing her and the kitten on the side of the bed, and waiting in silence while she cuddled her daughter and settled her down. 'Mummy needs a rest now, sweet-pea.' She rose as he spoke; she didn't think she could stand a repeat journey in his arms, but he frowned at her grimly before indicating Tiger. 'Hold that.' She did as she was told, and the next moment was being carried from the bedroom despite murmured protests. 'Shut up, Lydia.' He felt, rather than saw, his way downstairs and once in the lounge proceeded to bathe her head, very gently, before phoning the doctor. That accomplished, he disappeared into the kitchen again and re-emerged with two cups of strong sweet tea.

She was mesmerised by the unusual and dangerously sweet feeling of being looked after for once, and petrified that he would begin to ask questions about Matthew now they were alone. He didn't. He talked softly and inconsequentially about a hundred and one things until the doctor arrived. Wolf let him into the lounge and watched silently while his friend examined her head and established the facts.

'Nothing to worry about, but I'd like you to take it easy for the next day or two.' The good-looking, warm-eyed man smiled down at her gently. 'You're going to feel a trifle sore in the morning, with a head that will be worse than any hang-over you've ever had.'

'I've never had one,' she replied honestly.

'Is that so?' The professional smile faltered just a little and then recovered magnificently. 'I wish I could say the same. I'd rather there was someone around for the next twenty-four hours to keep an eye on you. Is there someone——?'

'I'll sort it, Andrew,' Wolf had cut in before she could open her mouth. 'She won't be alone.'

'Right.' Andrew smiled at her again before leaving the room with Wolf, and she heard the two of them talking quietly in the tiny hall before the front door opened and closed.

'I hope that sofa is comfortable.' As he re-entered the room she saw he had pulled his tie loose again, and despised herself for the way the fact registered hot and warm in her lower stomach.

'What?' She stared at him bewilderedly.

'The sofa.' He smiled slowly. 'If I'm going to spend the night on it I'd prefer a bit of comfort.'

'You can't.' The reply was instinctive, and as his face closed against her she desperately tried to take away the sharpness in her reaction. 'Please, we have to phone my mother,' she gabbled quickly. 'She would never forgive me if I didn't let her know the situation, Wolf, believe me, and she's used to sleeping over the odd night.' He couldn't sleep here, he just couldn't; the idea was somehow totally immoral.

'You don't think it would be kinder to let her have a good night's sleep and phone in the morning?' His voice was expressionless and cool, his eyes hooded.

'No.' She was quite unaware of how frightened her voice sounded. 'If you could ring her and explain? I know she'd want to come over.'

'The number?' His voice was curt, but softened considerably as he talked with her mother for a few moments, his tone reassuring.

'I'll stay until she arrives.' She didn't want him to but didn't dare object, and as he walked over to the chair opposite her and seated himself comfortably in its depths, crossing one muscled leg over the other as he leant back and surveyed her through narrowed eyes, she felt her nerves jump painfully.

'Is it true you've never had a hang-over?' he asked suddenly, his voice quiet. He could believe it, he thought tightly. That air of shy vulnerability, the almost tangible innocence—— He caught himself abruptly. But she wasn't, was she? There was living proof upstairs of the fact that she was a married woman who knew the facts of life, and that day in the lift... He felt the hardening in his loins that always accompanied the memory, despite his efforts to erase it. She had melted for him. And Mike Wilson... Exactly how well did she know him? And was it merely coincidence that she had arrived in his office or——? He stopped his thoughts grimly. Hell, this wouldn't do him any good, he'd better get out of here as soon as he could...

'I don't drink.' She looked tired and bruised and he didn't like the way it touched him. 'I don't like the taste,' she admitted quietly, her voice soft and shaky.

'You don't?' He adjusted his position in the chair and noticed the way her body tensed. He made her nervous. Or was it that she was frightened of men in general? Had this husband of hers abused her? He was surprised at the murderous rage the thought provoked. He definitely needed to get out of here...

'You'd better get to bed,' he said abruptly as he rose and took the two empty cups into the kitchen. 'Your mother will be here in a couple of minutes or so. I'll let her in and then disappear. Can you manage the stairs or shall I help you?' His voice was suddenly brusque and distant.

'I'll be fine,' she said quietly.

'OK. Goodnight, Lydia.' It was a clear dismissal.

Now what? she thought, as hurt mingled with anger. Suddenly he was the ice-man again, infinitely cold. She rose slowly and walked hesitantly to the kitchen where he was rinsing the cups under the tap. 'Thank you, Wolf.'

'For what?' He turned, his big body taut and his face cool, and she shrugged helplessly, finding words difficult.

'For coming round, for helping.'

'Forget it.' He smiled, but it didn't reach his eyes. 'I'd do the same for anyone. Take a couple of days off and I'll see you next week, OK?' He turned away, his body tense.

She stared at him a moment longer and then nodded quietly before turning and leaving the room, but the big body didn't move until he heard her footsteps upstairs, and then he leant against the sink with his arms outstretched as he forced his body to relax. Dammit, he didn't need this. If there was one thing he didn't need it was this.

It was some minutes later when Lydia heard the sound of her mother's key in the lock and then her voice talking with Wolf briefly, and again her stomach clenched with nerves.

As she heard the front door quietly close and then the sound of his car starting in the street below Lydia twisted miserably in the big bed. Her head was pounding in spite of the pills the doctor had given her and her whole body felt as though a herd of cows had been trampling on it, but the weight of her conscience made the physical afflictions unimportant. *She should have told him.* She curled up into a small ball as her mind ground on. Somehow this thing seemed to have snowballed and it was all her fault. Hot tears pricked against the back of her eyes and she sniffed disconsolately. He had been so kind in spite of the fact that he had obviously wanted to be elsewhere. She remembered his stony face in the kitchen and sighed wretchedly. She'd ruined his evening ... Had he been going to see Elda? The thought brought her abruptly upwards in the bed and a flush of hot pain speared her brain as her mother tapped carefully on the bedroom door.

'How are you feeling?'

'More embarrassed than anything at causing such a fuss,' Lydia replied quietly. 'Thanks for coming, Mum.' They talked for a few moments before her mother went downstairs to make herself a cup of cocoa, and then she was alone with her thoughts again, thoughts she just couldn't control. Thoughts that centred around the feel of his body as he had carried her close to him, his strong muscled arms and broad chest... She closed her eyes tightly and prayed for control, but it was difficult with the smell of his aftershave still clinging to her hair where she had rested her head against his face. And he was probably with Elda now.

At that thought the tears that had been held at bay by sheer will-power began to trickle from beneath her closed eyelids, soon to become a flood and then the flood a torrent. She should never have gone to work for him, it just wasn't working out. He had been so strange tonight: helping her, taking care of things, but overall that sense of cool aloofness, of cold reserve was what she remembered most, despite his gentleness. He had helped her because it had been the right thing to do in his eyes, that was all. She felt suddenly that he didn't even like her very much. And if she told him Matthew had been dead for three years? That she had deliberately misled him in order to secure the job as his secretary? She cringed mentally. He'd be absolutely livid and rightly so. Her mouth twisted in self-contempt. What was that ditty she'd learnt at Hannah's age? 'Oh, what a tangled web we weave when first we practise to deceive.' She hadn't known how true it was, she reflected miserably.

She pictured his face, eyes blazing and mouth tight with rage, and knew she didn't have the courage to tell him the truth. It was her last coherent thought before sleep overcame her.

CHAPTER FOUR

'LYDIA?' As she heard Wolf's deep voice on the other end of the phone she forced herself to take a steadying breath before she attempted to reply.

'Yes?' She didn't acknowledge that she recognised his voice; she couldn't, somehow.

'It's Wolf.' The tone was pleasant and cool, with just the right amount of polite concern that was fitting for an employer to an employee. 'I trust you're feeling considerably better this morning? I expected your mother to answer the phone.'

'I'm fine, thank you.' She didn't mention she had persuaded her mother to leave once breakfast was over. Wolf was the type of man to whom twenty-four hours meant twenty-four hours, and she had the feeling he wouldn't be too pleased at her flouting the doctor's advice, but years ago, just after Matthew's death, the two women had decided that if their close relationship was going to hold fast it was necessary that each understood they had to lead totally independent lives while still being available for each other when the need arose. Today was her mother's bridge morning and there was no good reason why she should miss a little event she looked forward to all week. 'It was good of you to help out last night,' she added carefully.

'No problem.' There was a brief pause. 'I'll see you on Monday morning, then.'

'I could come in tomorrow if you like, there's no——'

'Monday morning.' His voice was abrupt, and for an instant she pictured him at his desk, hard blue eyes narrowed and mouth straight. Her heart did a strange little somersault and she bit on her lower lip hard. The man seemed to get under her skin with no effort and it was most disconcerting, especially as she didn't affect him at all. 'There is absolutely no point in you pushing yourself when it isn't necessary,' he continued calmly. 'It might mean you have to have more time off in the long run.'

'I suppose so,' she agreed quietly. 'It's just that there are one or two important items of correspondence I was going to do first thing. That addition to the report, for instance——'

'It's already been dealt with.' His tone was not unkind but it brought home to her how little he really needed her. Anyone would do. Any reasonably capable secretary. She felt her heart thud painfully. For goodness' sake pull yourself together and stop being so pathetic, Lydia, she told herself angrily.

'Is there——?' He stopped abruptly and then continued in an almost expressionless voice. 'Is there anything you need over the weekend? Anything you'd like me to drop in?'

If only he was offering because he cared in some way rather than through a sense of duty, she thought painfully. But he had made it perfectly clear the last few minutes he was in the house that she was at best an irritation, at worst a burden. She wouldn't ask him for a thing.

'No, thank you.' She tried to sound as impersonal and brisk as she could, considering the sound of his voice was sending her insides whirling. 'Everything's under control.'

'I'm sure it is.' His voice was dry now and very distant. 'You are a very independent lady, aren't you?'

'Am I?' There was a note of surprise in her voice. 'I suppose I am,' she added quietly, unsure of how to react.

'Very independent and very single-minded,' the sardonic voice continued. 'A formidable combination, if I may say so. Goodbye, Lydia.'

'Goodbye,' she said quietly, unaware of the forlorn note in her soft voice. There was a split second of hesitation and then the phone was replaced at the other end, leaving her with a monotonous buzz to say the call had ended.

The weekend dragged by on leaden feet, but then it seemed as though Monday morning had arrived too fast as she got ready for work, her stomach churning. She pulled a few strands of her hair forward, cutting it in a soft fringe to hide the cut on her forehead, and outwardly at least no sign of the accident was showing as she walked into the office later. Inwardly the whole incident, or more correctly Wolf's part in it, had affected her far more than she cared to admit. Hannah had plagued her all weekend with requests to see 'the nice man' again, and in the finish she had had to be uncharacteristically sharp with her small daughter to get her to stop, which had then resulted in a massive guilt session.

All in all, everything seems wrong, she thought silently as she hung her coat carefully in the corner of the room, but for no good reason. Or nothing she cared to explore, anyway.

'Good morning.' She hadn't heard the connecting door open, but now as she swung round it was to find Wolf framed in the doorway of his room, a polite smile stitched on an otherwise cold face. 'Fully recovered?' he asked coolly.

'Yes, thank you,' she nodded quickly, annoyed to find she had blushed scarlet and that her pulses had leapt so violently at the sight of him that her heart had run away like an express train. 'Is there anything urgent you'd like me to attend to first?'

'Plenty.' He nodded drily towards her in-tray in which several tapes lay, before turning into his own office and shutting the door. She stared after him as a little curl of angry irritation snaked a path into her mind. So. That was how things stood: no softening of the rigid ice-cool image, nothing approaching even the mildest form of friendship. Fine, just fine. She wasn't here to make friends, after all, she was here to do a job. And she'd make sure he found no fault with her work.

The thought carried her furiously through the day on such a burst of adrenalin that she accomplished an exorbitant amount of work before replacing the cover on her word processor just after five. Wolf had spoken, when necessary, in polite monosyllables which she had answered in like vein, and it wasn't until she was waiting for the tube among a crowd of London commuters that she realised a tension headache was drumming away at the back of her eyes. 'Is it worth it?' she murmured faintly to herself as she rubbed a tired hand across her eyes, opening them to find a portly, well-dressed businessman surveying her with distinct apprehension before edging away down the platform a little. Talking to herself out loud! This was all she needed. But perhaps tomorrow would be better.

It wasn't, nor the next day, nor the next. For some reason the cool, careful formality with which Wolf had always treated her had turned into a cold abruptness that

she was at a loss to understand. She hadn't *meant* to fall
off the darn ladder! She found herself gnawing at the
thought in her lunch-hour on the Friday as she did some
shopping, wandering round the large supermarket close
to Wolf's office-block without seeing the well-stocked
shelves in front of her. Was he mad because she'd in-
terfered with his precious work schedule? But she'd
caught up that first day, or very nearly. And she would
have come in before Monday if he hadn't vetoed it so
firmly. He had to be the most impossible, awkward, in-
tractable man...

She returned to the office with an empty shopping-
basket and a deep frown to find Wolf's door firmly shut
and that unmistakable throaty giggle deep inside. Elda.
The sinking feeling in the pit of her stomach that went
hand in hand with the name did an immediate nose-dive.
The elegant brunette had already rung twice this week.
What on earth did she want, anyway? As if you didn't
know, she told herself grimly as she started work again,
tapping the silent computer keys with unnecessary vigour.
As if you didn't know...

'Lydia, I'm just popping out for a quick lunch——
Are you all right?' Wolf stopped dead in the middle of
her office with Elda hanging on his arm, and she hastily
tried to school her features into something approaching
normality. But somehow, as they had left his room, she'd
had the strangest feeling that someone had punched her
hard in the stomach.

'Of course.' She smiled stiffly but it was the best she
could do. 'Have a good lunch.'

'Elda, I'll be down in a moment.' As Wolf disen-
tangled himself from Elda's grasp Lydia saw the beautiful
brunette's fine, pencil-thin eyebrows raise themselves a
fraction, the blue eyes narrowing thoughtfully before she

walked out of the office, shutting the door quietly behind her.

'Something's happened, hasn't it? Is it Matthew?' Wolf moved to stand just in front of her and for a moment the desire to stand up and hit him hard across the face was so strong she could actually taste it. How dared he stand there and pretend he had any interest in her situation one way or the other? How dared he! One minute he had Elda hanging on his arm like a limpet and the next—— The flood of unreasonable, unjust rage was immediately swamped by cold hard reason. He was her *boss*, for goodness' sake. Of course he would care that she might be less than the perfectly efficient, one hundred percent operational machine he was used to. The thought didn't help.

'It's nothing.' Her smile was brittle and the sharp blue eyes watching her narrowed thoughtfully. 'It won't affect my work and——'

'Damn your work!' The words were an explosion and for a moment the stillness that followed was absolute. 'Lydia, do you need someone to talk to? I mean——' He stopped abruptly and seemed to collect himself before continuing. 'There are counselling places for situations like this. Have you considered——?'

'I don't want to talk to anyone.' She lowered her head as she spoke—that blue gaze was unnerving—and missed the tiny instinctive movement he took towards her before it was firmly checked. He thought she was cracking up, was that it?

'I see.' There was a moment of silence and then he spoke again, his words bringing her head sharply upwards, her eyes angry. 'Have you considered Hannah in all this? It might be a form of indulgence to try and get through by yourself.'

He did think she was cracking up, she thought tersely. He didn't credit her with any guts at all.

'I always put Hannah first in everything I do.' She glared at him furiously even as she acknowledged that from his viewpoint it was a reasonable comment. She had to tell him. Now. Before she lost her nerve. 'Actually there is something I have to tell you——'

'Wolf, the taxi's waiting.' The words died on her lips as Elda's dark head peered round the door. 'I'm sorry, but I really can't be late for that appointment at two...' The big blue eyes were prettily penitent.

For a moment Lydia thought Wolf was going to snap at the lovely brunette as his head swung round and his eyes narrowed into slits of ice, but then he took a deep breath, that iron control she had seen so often in the last few weeks springing into place, and when he spoke his voice was pleasant, if cool. 'OK, Elda, don't fret.' He moved across and took the other woman's arm, gently turning her round and out of the doorway. 'I'll be back at two,' he said over his shoulder to Lydia. 'We'll continue this conversation then.' The door shut with a firm, cool click.

Over my dead body. She stared at the closed door bleakly. Definitely over my dead body. The moment had come and gone and she just wouldn't have the courage to admit the truth with no lead-in. Besides which, what if he should subsequently ask why she had been looking so wretched when he and Elda had left his office? What could she say then? That she was jealous? The thought shocked her into an immediate denial. She wasn't. Of course she wasn't. How could she be jealous of someone she didn't even like? She bit her lip hard. She might find him physically attractive but that was all, and no doubt there were hundreds of men who were just as attractive ut normal human beings as well. Not blocks of ice. And he *had* wanted an efficient, capable secretary for a few months. Which she was. That was all that mattered to him. She sank back in her seat despondently. So why did she feel so horribly guilty?

When Wolf returned just before two she lowered her head immediately to her work after a cursory good afternoon, her cheeks flushing scarlet, hoping he'd let the matter drop.

'I'd like a word in my office, please, Lydia.'

She didn't move as he strode across the room but as he opened his door she spoke quickly, her voice steady. 'If it's about what was said earlier, I'd rather not.' She raised her head slowly.

He turned with his hand on the door-handle, his big body taut and straight and his eyes cold. 'What was said earlier? I wasn't aware anything *was* said. That is precisely——'

'And I think it's best that way. I'm sorry.' A faint trace of Elda's heavy, musky perfume had come into the room with him and that, combined with the oblique sarcasm in his dark voice, strengthened her resolve.

'I see.' He eyed her grimly. 'And if I think differently?'

She stared at him, faintly nonplussed. 'Well, why should you?' She gestured towards the word processor in front of her. 'My work isn't suffering and my private life is my own concern. I only work here and that's temporary——'

'I'm well aware of that!' The words had been a sharp bark and his eyes glittered dangerously for one long moment before she saw him take an almost visible control on his temper. 'You do understand I can't afford your concentration to be anything less than one hundred per cent?' he asked stiffly, after a long taut moment of silence.

'Yes.' She stared up at him, trying to keep calm. 'And I've already said that my work isn't suffering.'

'I heard you.' He glared at her as though she had just admitted to some heinous crime. 'But would you accept that you aren't the best judge of that at the moment?' He raised his hand as she went to reply, his face autocratic. 'It is well known that a marriage breakdown causes the sort of stress that is only a little less than a bereavement. You might feel you're coping fine, but surely to talk to someone else, an independent stranger if you like, wouldn't do any harm? If only to find out exactly what you do want.'

'There is no need.' She called on every shred of willpower she possessed and managed a bright, dismissive smile which in the face of his dark frown was Oscar-winning stuff. 'I've told you I'm all right and I am— Hannah too. I've been used to coping with things on my own for some time now.' That much at least was true. 'The last few weeks haven't changed anything.'

He opened his mouth to reply just as the telephone rang shrilly by her side, and never had she been more pleased at an interruption. She whisked it up before he could say a word, her face as blank as she could make it. 'Good afternoon. Mr Strade's secretary speaking.'

'Is he there?' The husky female voice didn't bother to identify itself but it didn't matter. Lydia would have recognised it anywhere. 'I've left my gloves in his office.'

'It's Elda.' She raised cool eyes to his. 'Missing gloves?' He swore, softly but vehemently, and strode into his office.

Wonderful. She sat quite still as the heavy thudding of her heart began to settle. Absolutely wonderful. No amount of money was worth this.

The rest of the afternoon passed in comparative peace for the simple reason that Wolf didn't step out of his office once and she didn't venture in. At exactly five o'clock she slipped the cover on the word processor and left an impressive pile of finished work at the side of it. She was going home now and nothing was going to stop her. She'd had enough. He'd probably berate her on Monday because she hadn't taken the work in but she couldn't, she just couldn't. She needed at least forty-eight hours to charge up her batteries before she faced him again.

The lift doors were just closing when she heard his voice. 'Hold it.'

It was reflex action that made her keep the doors open for him, but as he stepped into the lift with a brief nod of thanks she wished she hadn't. He was dressed in a black dinner-jacket, the dusky red shirt and silk bow tie enhancing his tanned skin and black hair, and the superb cut of the jacket making his broad shoulders even broader. He looked devastating. Devastating and over-whelmingly attractive, and she felt her knees grow weak. This wasn't fair, it just wasn't fair. Damn that little washroom. 'Thanks.' She noticed he was still carrying his briefcase despite the evening wear, and suddenly the remembrance of the last time she had been in a lift with him turned her face crimson. 'I'm already late,' he added with a slight frown.

'Going somewhere nice?' She forced the words through numb lips and was surprised at how normal her voice sounded. What was happening to her? She didn't

want to feel like this; it was making a mockery of ev
thing she had thought she was.

'A somewhat boring reception.' He smiled briefly. 'Bu.
then to the opera, so the whole evening won't be a total
disaster.' He glanced at his watch before speaking again.
'I can drop you off on the way—it's in the right
direction.'

'There's no need——'

The blue eyes fastened on her, a dark, satirical gleam
in their depths, and her voice trailed away. 'I can drop
you off on the way,' he repeated quietly, his voice silky
with an underlying thread of iron.

A gust of rain, the drops needle-sharp and icy, met
their faces as they left the warmth of the building, and
as Lydia slid into Wolf's Mercedes she was aware of a
small feeling of relief that she hadn't got to fight her
way home with the rest of the commuters on such a filthy
night. It vanished instantly as he joined her in the car,
the enclosed confines of the beautiful vehicle bringing
him much too close for comfort. She glanced at him
under her eyelashes as he manoeuvred into a place in
the fast-flowing traffic. The dark hair was slicked back
and he looked as though he'd just shaved; who had he
gone to so much trouble for? She was immediately
furious with herself for thinking such a thing. It was
none of her business, and what did it matter? He was
just her boss, after all.

He drove swiftly and competently through the cold
London night as the rain beat a steady tattoo on the
windscreen, the wipers labouring to clear the window at
times as sudden squalls threw gusts of hail in their path.
The silence between them lengthened but she felt quite
unable to break it, and he seemed to be in a world of

own, his eyes concentrating on the road ahead and s mouth tight and grim.

'Thank you.' As they drew up outside her house she turned to him, forcing a smile on her face. 'I hope you have a good time tonight.'

'I will.' He didn't smile back. 'It's guaranteed.'

'Guaranteed?' And then the penny dropped. 'Oh, it's someone special, then?' Elda. She might have known.

'Someone . . .' His eyes narrowed as if in puzzlement and then cleared abruptly. 'Not exactly, Lydia, no. But the company I shall be with know how to enjoy themselves. That is a prerequisite if they expect me to attend.'

She stared at him, her eyes darkening at the harshness in his tone. He sounded angry with her, and after the miserable week she'd had she fired back without stopping to consider her words. 'By company I take it you mean women?' She raised her chin as she met the ice-blue gaze head on.

'If I had meant women I would have said so,' he said coldly, 'but, as it happens, I do expect my female companions to be good company, yes. When I acquire a good suit I don't mind going to some lengths to make sure the measurements are right and the cloth suitable, and I pay for the best, but having done all that I expect it to be on time, precisely to my requirements and prepared to fit me exactly.'

She couldn't believe her ears. '*A suit?*' The rain still continued to drum down on the roof of the car but neither of them was aware of the outside world as they faced each other like two gladiators about to enter the ring. 'We're talking about a man and woman relationship here, not a cut-and-dried purchase of an expendable item.'

'Isn't it the same thing?' His face and voice were perfectly expressionless but the piercing eyes were watching her intently, their blueness as sharp as glass.

'Are you telling me...?' Her voice faltered. He couldn't be saying what she thought he was saying. Not a man like him. Handsome, inordinately wealthy, with the world, or his own part of it at least, at his feet. It was ludicrous. 'Are you saying you pay for your women?' she asked faintly.

'Of course not.' He was instantly and angrily scathing. 'Not in the way you mean.' He eyed her sardonically, his lip curling at her confusion. 'But what I *do* mean is that the females of my acquaintance expect to be wined and dined in some... comfort, escorted to all the right places—you know the routine.'

'I don't, actually.' She was sitting very straight in her seat now, her cheeks fiery but her eyes steady as they watched his face. 'And I'm very glad I don't.'

'Oh, come on, Lydia,' he drawled lazily, with a small, mocking smile that didn't reach his eyes. 'You are a very beautiful and desirable woman and I'm sure you must have had lots of men-friends before you married your husband. Are you telling me you didn't get the most out of them you could?'

'Now, just hang on a minute,' she interrupted frostily as a flood of burning hot rage swept through her small frame. 'Just hang on a darn minute! Don't you dare make assumptions about me, Wolf Strade.' She forgot he was her boss, forgot all the normal social niceties such a relationship warranted, as her eyes filled with rage and her body became as taut as a bow. 'Matthew was my first and only boyfriend, as it happened. We grew up together from children, and if you expect me to apologise for that you've got another think coming.'

Lydia——'

But she was in no mood to listen and swept on, her next words hardening the face that had softened at her admission. 'It sounds to me as if you get exactly what you deserve in your relationships. If all you're interested in is someone to grace your table and your bed, a live doll with the right connections, not to mention proportions—— '

'I merely choose women of like mind,' he interrupted coldly, 'who are happy with no commitment, no ties.'

'No, you don't.' He stiffened at the challenge, but she was too angry to notice. 'You *choose* women who are shallow and materialistic, who have no real values. That's what you do.' Her eyes were flashing fire. 'Your earlier comments when you lumped the whole female sex together in one greedy package prove that! And what on earth is with this "choosing" idea, anyway? Women aren't clothes that you can select at will and wear for a time before you dispose of them—not *real* women. But if you only shop in the tinsel and glitter department that is all you're going to see, isn't it? A real relationship isn't a matter of choosing in the way you mean, with one person selecting another like a lump of meat.'

'You're being ridiculous.' His voice was deadly cold.

'You didn't like it when I thought you paid for your women, but really that's exactly what you do,' she said slowly. 'All the time. Not with money, nothing as crude as that, but with the places you take them so they can be seen, the presents and attention they take as their right, even your performance in bed. You pay, Wolf. Don't fool yourself.' She stared him straight in the eyes, her cheeks scarlet.

'My *performance* in bed?' He hadn't liked that a bit, she could tell from the way his face hardened almost savagely. 'So you think I give a performance, do you?'

As he leant over her the warm, clean fragrance of his skin mingled with the intoxicating sensuality of his aftershave and she felt her senses begin to spin even before his mouth came down on hers. She had expected anger, violence, but the moment his lips touched hers she realised this was a deliberate assault on her senses, a subtle form of punishment for her condemning words but one she was powerless to resist. The kiss was more teasing than penetrating...at first. She could have moved away—he wasn't holding her, after all, his mouth just lightly resting on hers—but it wasn't until much later that she realised the idea had never even occurred to her. And then the kiss became more demanding, his tongue exploring the soft contours of her lips and mouth and causing tiny helpless shivers to shudder down her spine. She had never guessed it could be like this... The same emotions she had felt that day in the lift returned to torment her. She was twenty-seven years of age, had a small daughter who was all her own, and yet it was as though she had never been kissed before in her life. The thought had the power to jerk her away from Wolf as though she had been burnt. How could she betray Matthew's memory like that? And with a man like Wolf Strade? And especially after what he had just said?

'Lydia——'

As she wrenched open the door and stumbled out of the car she heard him call to her, but she sped across the street and up the steps to the house without a backward glance, thrusting her key into the lock and almost falling into the small hall as though it were a real

...f that was after her, fangs open for the kill and hard
...llow eyes dilated.

How had that happened? She looked dazedly into the
small mirror in the bathroom some minutes later, after
a furious bout of weeping, and sniffed dismally. Hannah
would be home soon. She had gone to tea with Sophie,
and Sophie's mother was dropping her home just after
half past six. She had to pull herself together and act
normally. She'd think about this later.

But when later came, in the quiet and solitude of her
lonely bed, she was no nearer to an answer. All she knew
was that from the moment she had laid eyes on Wolf
Strade her world had turned upside-down, and her with
it. She wasn't the person she had known for twenty-seven
years; there was some other being working there inside
her skin. A passionate, tempestuous, strange being with
hidden desires and cravings that the old Lydia found
more than a little shocking. It didn't help that the rest
of the female population seemed to find him equally attractive. She remembered a conversation she had over-
heard the week before when she had been sitting quietly
in the canteen one lunchtime. Two of the junior secretaries had been seated at a table just round the corner
from her, and although she wasn't visible to their gaze
every word they had spoken had registered loud and
clear.

'He's such an out-and-out dish.' A deep sigh had followed the statement, along with the sound of chairs being
pulled out, and Lydia had grimaced sympathetically for
whoever had spoken. They'd certainly got it bad! There
had been a wealth of hunger in the female voice. Boyfriend trouble, perhaps?

'I know.' The other girl had added her sigh. 'But
there's no way he'd look at me or you, Carol.'

'Well, I can dream, can't I?' the first voice had said, a little indignantly.

'By all means, dream on, but as far as I know he's never dated an employee—not his style.'

'Well, with the women he can have at his beck and call, it's not to be wondered at, is it?' the said Carol had replied tersely. 'Did you see that photo in the paper a few months back. "Wolf Strade and friend", the caption said. Some friend! With a figure like she'd got I bet they didn't play ludo all night.' A small, suggestive giggle had followed.

'*Carol*!'

'Well... It makes me mad. Why can't men see that ordinary working girls can be fun too?' Carol had said petulantly.

'You're getting positively sour in your old age,' the other voice had said laughingly. 'And anyway, he'd be too much for you to handle. He was married once, you know, and since then he's had more women than I've had hot dinners, if only a quarter of the rumours about him are true.'

'Oh, they'd be true,' Carol had sighed resignedly. 'You've only to look into those beautiful blue eyes to know they'd be true, and frankly I'd be prepared to let him teach me anything, *anything* he knows.'

Lydia had left the canteen at that point but the women's conversation had stayed with her all day, try as she might to dismiss it from her mind, and even now she could remember every word. It was stupid and irrational and quite out of character, but she had felt like slapping both of them, and that had horrified her almost as much as the fact that she had sat and listened to a private conversation. *Had* he been married? she wondered fretfully. And, if so, how had it ended and where was his ex now? What was the matter with her? She shook herself angrily. It was none of her business, *it wasn't*.

But *why* had he kissed her? She twisted restlessly in the big bed. Did he think she was easy, like some of the other women who threw themselves at him so blatantly? Well, she'd hardly done anything to dissuade him from such a line of thought, she reminded herself miserably.

She had returned the kiss until the very last moment. She knew it and he would have known it. He hadn't been holding her, trapping her in any way; she had been perfectly free to move away if she'd so wished. But she hadn't! The thought brought on a fresh deluge of humiliation and she sat up to punch her pillows violently into shape.

This couldn't continue. She'd be a nervous wreck if she worked for him much longer. The thought gathered steam as she lay there in the soft darkness, and by the time she drifted into a restless, troubled sleep her mind was made up.

She was leaving Strade Engineering and she would tell him so first thing on Monday morning. Desperate situations needed desperate measures, and right now that was exactly how she felt—desperate.

CHAPTER FIVE

LYDIA dressed very carefully for work the following Monday, choosing a demure high-necked blouse in pale coffee and a calf-length full skirt in a darker shade, securing her hair in a tight French plait that she fixed with grim fierceness, and allowing herself just the merest touch of eyeshadow on her wide eyelids. There. She checked herself in the mirror just before she left to take Hannah to nursery. He couldn't say there was the remotest suggestion of a come-on in this chaste ensemble. She had tormented herself all weekend with the thought that she might have encouraged him in some way, although in all honesty she couldn't see how. But she intended to be all cool efficiency this morning, composed and calm when she told him she would be leaving at the end of the week. Her stomach turned over at the thought. Stop it, she told herself silently. Wolf Strade will be like a shadowy dream in a few months, an indistinct, vague phantom relegated firmly to the past.

The vague phantom was prowling about her office when she arrived some time later, a sheaf of papers in his hand and a ferocious scowl on his face. 'I've been here all weekend.' He glared at her as if it were her fault. 'Those fools in my Scotland office have nearly lost us the biggest order we've ever had through sheer incompetence. Can you be ready to leave in a couple of hours?'

'Leave?' She stared at him as though he were mad.

'For Scotland.' He gestured irritably as though she were being deliberately obtuse. 'If I don't salvage this thing now, in the next twenty-four hours, I can kiss over five million pounds goodbye.'

It was an unfortunate choice of words, but even as she felt her cheeks burn she saw the import of the phrase hadn't registered with him at all. He was in business mode, all his energies concentrated on the job in hand and it was unlikely that he even remembered Friday evening. And for this she had been devastated all weekend? She glared back at him now as her thoughts brought sparks to her eyes. 'What time do you want to go?'

'Lunchtime.'

'Right.'

He hadn't even noticed her abruptness, she thought painfully as he strode back into his office, growling instructions about the pile of papers on her desk as he went. He was impossible. Absolutely impossible.

She phoned her mother, who assured her she would love to take care of Hannah for a few days, phoned the nursery to say she would be dropping in a little later to explain things to Hannah and say goodbye, and then worked frantically on the more urgent correspondence before taking it, and a cup of black coffee, in to him mid-morning. He was sitting at his desk as she entered the room, and looked tired to death.

'Coffee?' She indicated the cup as she placed the papers in front of him. 'You look as if you need it.'

'I don't know if I can pull this one round, Lydia.'

No. As she stared at his face, uncharacteristically doubtful and faintly boyish, she felt her heart thud painfully. Don't do this to me. Not now. Fury, temper, irritability she could cope with, but not this weariness that was putting a grey tinge of exhaustion on the handsome face and made her want to gather him up in

her arms and kiss all the anxiety away. Against that her
heart had no defence at all.

'You're tired,' she said as matter-of-factly as she could,
considering she was aching to give more than verbal re-
assurance. 'How much sleep have you had in the last
forty-eight hours, anyway?' she added reprovingly.

'Sleep?' He looked up at her as though she were talking
a foreign language. 'I've cat-napped once or twice, I
think.'

'And food?' She stared down at him severely. 'Have
you eaten?'

'Some sandwiches some time yesterday.' He had been
sipping the coffee as they talked and already a tinge of
the old mordant note was back in his voice. 'And don't
fuss, woman. I can't stand fussing.' He eyed her
sardonically.

'Nevertheless, you need someone to keep an eye on
you.' She smiled in what she hoped was a cool, sec-
retarial way, but he didn't smile back as he looked up
at her, the piercing eyes suddenly very clear and blue.

'No, I don't.' They both knew he was answering the
light comment with more seriousness than it had warranted. 'Some people aren't meant to form bonds, Lydia,
not even in the mildest sense. They walk through life
alone because they are a danger to themselves and other
people if they don't.'

'Do you think so?' She didn't know how to reply, what
to say, and was floundering badly.

'I know so.' He looked at her for one more long
moment and then lowered his head to the papers. 'Believe me, I *do* know so.'

'Oh.' As she stood looking down at his bent head an
almost irrepressible urge to ask more, to delve deeper,
brought her lips firmly clamping shut. She was his tem-

porary secretary, that was all, and he had just reminded her of it in the nicest way he could. Take it on board and be smart, she told herself silently, protect yourself. For all you know he is probably still in love with his ex-wife, despite all those other women.

'I'd like to say goodbye to Hannah before I leave for Scotland,' she said, after a few seconds of absolute silence. 'And of course I shall need to collect some clothes and things. How long do you think we'll be away?'

'Two or three days, four at the most.' He looked up and she saw his face was the old expressionless mask again, withdrawn and remote. 'And of course you must see Hannah. The flight is booked for two this afternoon but we need to be at the airport a little earlier. If you want to scoot off now and see to things, I'll pick you up just before one.'

She nodded and left the office without another word, but just as she was preparing to leave she picked up the internal phone on impulse and ordered a hot meal from the canteen to be brought up immediately. He might call it fussing, he might call it a lot worse, but he couldn't carry on at this pace without burning himself out. And she didn't want that. She checked the weakness quickly in her mind but it was no good. She was concerned about him even as she told herself it was foolish.

By half-past twelve she was packed and scribbling a short list of notes to her mother as she sat with a cup of coffee on the occasional table beside her and Tiger purring contentedly on her lap. Her mother had offered to stay at Lydia's house in order that Hannah's routine was interrupted as little as possible so there was little to organise. Hannah herself had accepted the news quite stoically in spite of it being the first time they had been parted since she was born. Several of her friends' parents were often away on business so the idea was not new to her, besides which the present Lydia had mentioned would be brought on her return had been a definite plus.

As Lydia glanced at the small suitcase by the door her lip curled in wry self-mockery. Dashing off to Scotland with him was a little different from her plans of the weekend! She shook her head at her own weakness. But she couldn't let him down in an emergency. There was time to tell him she intended to leave later, once they were back in London again.

His authoritative knock just before one set the butterflies whizzing frantically in her stomach and she took a long deep breath as she opened the door. 'Hi.' Was it her imagination or was he faintly sheepish? she asked herself silently as he walked through and picked up the small suitcase. 'Thanks for ordering the meal.' He put the suitcase down again and turned to face her, his eyes wary. 'And I never said I appreciate you responding so well to the emergency.'

'It comes with the job.' She hoped she looked cool and composed because she certainly didn't feel it. He seemed to have more personality changes in the space of an hour than the rest of the people she knew put together. 'You did warn me I might have to take off at a minute's notice at my interview,' she said lightly.

'Nevertheless, it was good of you.' He looked so gorgeous as he dominated her small lounge that she felt the blood positively pounding through her veins. 'Thank you.'

'No problem.' She smiled carefully.

'Did Hannah take the news of the trip OK?' he asked quietly as he looked at her steadily through clear silver-blue eyes.

'Fine.' She smiled carefully again, aiming for lightness. 'My mother is very good with her, they get on like a house on fire, so I never need to worry if I can't be with her.'

'That's good.' He eyed her soberly. 'It must be re-assuring for you to know she's in good hands.'

'It is.' She glanced at him, faintly puzzled. It was almost as though he was hesitating about something, but perhaps it was her imagination. She certainly couldn't trust her feelings around this man, that was for sure. 'There's no one like your own mother, after all.'

'I should imagine not.' The words were faintly enigmatic but she sensed he hadn't meant them to be.

'Do your parents live close by?' she asked quietly, feeling as though she was treading on thin ice. It would have been a normal, polite pleasantry with most people, but with Wolf the normal wasn't, somehow.

'My mother died in an accident when I was about eighteen months old, so unfortunately I can't remember anything of her,' he answered shortly, 'and my father lives in New Zealand. We communicate regularly, he's a great guy, but due to the distance we only meet a few times a year.' He shrugged dismissively.

'Oh...' Her tender heart was touched and it showed. 'That's a shame.' His face closed immediately, his mouth straightening.

'I've never looked at it that way.' It was a definite snub, but in view of the fact that he had just told her he'd lost his mother at such an early age, she found it washed over her head.

'Well, I would.' She looked him straight in the face now. 'I think families are important.'

'Do you?' He smiled slightly at her vehemence and she saw the hard face relax slightly. 'Well, I suppose I'm not the best judge of that. My mother was killed on an expedition my father had organised, and I think he always felt the fault was his. They were very much in love and it took him many years to get over her death. In the meantime I was cared for by a nanny and various servants in whatever country we happened to be in until I went to boarding-school in England at the age of eight. I never really got to know my father until just a few years ago when——' He stopped abruptly. 'When I was passing through a bad time,' he finished shortly. 'He was a tower of strength and we found we had more in common than we thought.'

'You must have travelled extensively, then, when you were younger?' She felt the personal revelations were alien to him and sat uncomfortably on his shoulders, and aimed at lightening the mood.

'And how.' He grinned suddenly and, as before, it did something to her heart that was acutely uncomfortable. 'But it had its advantages although I didn't appreciate them at the time. I can speak fluent French, German, Italian and Greek and have a smattering of several other languages, all directly attributable to my nomadic beginnings. Once I was taught languages officially at school I found I had absorbed far more in my early years than I had known.'

'That's good.' It hurt her, far, far more than it should have done, that he hadn't had a mother's love. Ridiculous, and he would be furious if he knew what she was thinking, but the thought of the boy Wolf being cared for by paid employees hit a nerve inside her that was distinctly painful.

'Did you enjoy school?' she asked as she slipped into her jacket, keeping her voice casual. He mustn't guess that these tiny glimpses into his personal life were of intense interest.

'Yes, I did, actually.' There was a note of surprise in his voice as though he imagined he shouldn't have. 'Most of the other boys were always aching to get home and see their folks, but as that didn't apply to me I found school life fulfilling and interesting. My father sent me to a good school and always provided the cash for any activities I wanted to take up.'

'Did he?' But he wasn't around, she thought painfully, for the childish confidences and sharing of troubles that were so important in adolescence. He had had to cope alone.

'What about you?' He smiled down at her and her heart flipped over. 'The regulation two-point-four family?' he asked teasingly.

'Almost.' She smiled back carefully. 'My parents just had me and the dog. They wanted more children but somehow, after me, it just didn't happen. Then Dad died when I was twelve and I guess from that point Matthew took over looking after me. He was brilliant to me and Mum,' she finished flatly. 'I'll never forget that.'

'Of course you won't.' His voice had stiffened but she didn't notice as she reached for her handbag. As she turned to him again he gestured towards a large framed photograph of herself and Matthew that she kept on a small coffee-table under the window at one end of the room. She had felt in the early days that it was important for Hannah to see and recognise her father as much as possible as she would never see him again, and the idea had worked well. When asked by another child at nursery why her Daddy never came to pick her up, Hannah answered quite cheerfully and without a moment's hesitation that her Daddy was in heaven and liked toast and marmalade for breakfast.

'Where did she get that last bit from?' the teacher who had reported the children's conversation had asked Lydia when she had arrived to pick Hannah up in the evening.

'That's *her* favourite breakfast,' Lydia had replied quietly, her eyes warm as she had watched her small daughter playing with a group of friends. She was secure and happy and contented. Matthew couldn't have wished for more. She hadn't failed him.

'Lydia?' She was brought back to the present with a jolt as she realised Wolf was looking straight at her, his mouth tight. 'Have you seen him recently?'

'Seen him . . . ?' The suddenness of the question flummoxed her completely. 'Matthew? No . . .'

'And is there any chance of the two of you getting back together again?' he asked, still in the strange, blank, hard voice as he watched her tightly through cool blue eyes.

'Wolf——'

'Just answer yes or no, Lydia.' His eyes were totally expressionless and as blue as a summer sky. 'Is there a chance?'

'No.' She took a deep breath. 'But——'

'We've got to go.' He picked up the suitcase and strode to the door, waiting for her to precede him. 'We're going to cut it fine and we need to be on that flight.'

He had known she was going to talk about Matthew and he hadn't wanted her to, but why not? Lydia asked herself bemusedly as she walked out into the street to see a taxi-cab waiting patiently. Why ask her about him like that if he didn't want her to explain? But then he wouldn't want to get involved, would he? His earlier words about relationships flooded her mind. If he could ascertain that his temporary secretary wasn't likely to have any difficult emotional outbursts that might affect her capability, if he could be reasonably sure that the estranged husband wasn't likely to cause problems with his efficient machine... That was all he was interested in, after all. The grey day outside suddenly seemed a shade greyer. But why had he kissed her? Once seated in the taxi Wolf sat staring silently out of the window and she glanced at the hard profile under her lashes. He was an enigma. She felt a moment of deep and painful confusion. She had never met anyone she understood less.

Once the formalities were completed they were settled comfortably on the plane and she couldn't fault Wolf's courtesy in the way he treated her but... it was so cold. Chillingly so.

And in the taxi, the departure lounge, and now here on the plane, he was so very careful not to touch her, to make sure that not a part of his body came into contact with hers.

'Wolf?' She touched his arm to get his attention and felt powerful muscles tense under her hand. 'Have I done something to annoy you? Recently, that is...' She smiled carefully as she kept her voice light. Observation of this man over the last few weeks had shown her that any display of emotion, however slight, was met with an expressionless mask.

'Annoy?' He turned to her, his face cool and hard and his mouth cynical as he prepared to make an easy rejoinder, but as he did so blue eyes met soft, velvety brown ones and the words seemed to die in his throat as their gaze joined and held. She could feel herself begin to drown in the silver-blue sea of his eyes as time hung suspended in a sapphire mist, the thud of her heart and pounding of the blood through her veins the only things that convinced her this was happening. And then his face came slowly closer, as though something outside himself had control over his actions, and his warm lips brushed tantalisingly over her half-open mouth, their touch provocative. 'So soft and beautiful...' She could barely hear the murmured words, and the next instant he had settled back into his own seat, his eyes shadowed and unfathomable. 'You haven't annoyed me, Lydia.' She had forgotten her original question and blinked at him in surprise before she pulled herself together. He was dangerous. Oh, he was so, so dangerous.

'Good.' She smiled brightly and forced herself to reach forward and select a magazine from the pile the efficient blonde stewardess had brought her a few minutes before. 'That's all right, then.' She hoped the trembling that had spread into every fibre of her body wasn't visible to those sharp, ice-blue eyes but as she glanced at him, the brittle smile held in place by sheer will-power, she saw he was reaching for his briefcase, his face distant and preoccupied as though he had forgotten her already. She knew a moment's deep and humiliating chagrin at how easily he dismissed her, before a fierce flare of pride brought her chin upwards. The light caress didn't mean anything to her either, *it didn't*. She wouldn't let it.

They were met at the airport by Wolf's general manager of the Scottish branch, a tall, good-looking man called Douglas Webb, who immediately began to apologise, once introductions were over, for the imminent catastrophe.

'Calm yourself, Doug.' Wolf's attitude surprised Lydia. She had expected tight rage or the icy-cold, biting condemnation he was so good at, but as the three of them walked towards the waiting car his face was cool but friendly, his voice even. 'It's not a *fait accompli* yet, by a long way.'

'If you want my resignation——'

'Of course I don't want your resignation,' Wolf responded with his usual acerbity. 'What I *want* is for the two of us to work together and get out of this mess. I had copies of the costings and production dates too, Doug, and I didn't pick it up either, although the way the facts were buried it isn't surprising. You trusted Mike Wilson to give you the correct data—hell, *I* trusted him! It looks like we've all been had,' he finished grimly, his mouth hard.

'I heard you got rid of him.' The other man's voice was almost faint with relief. Lydia guessed he had not expected his chairman to be so reasonable.

'A little too late, by the look of it.' Wolf slanted a sideways look at Lydia's face as they reached the car, and as their eyes met she flushed slightly, remembering her earlier protestations that he was being too hard on Mike. If this important deal was lost through Mike Wilson's dishonesty, even a prison sentence didn't seem too severe. She still found it hard to take in that Anna's husband was little more than a crook.

'Why did he do it?' Doug Webb asked. 'I mean, he had everything going for him——'

'Filthy lucre.' Wolf's voice was grim. 'He got greedy.'

They drove straight to the office and spent several hours there, and by seven o'clock in the evening Lydia was again reflecting that Wolf Strade was an extraordinary man. In spite of practically no sleep in the last forty-eight hours, his mind was still razor-sharp, the intimidating intelligence and hard practical business acumen unaffected. The air had become electric as soon as he had walked through the door of Strade Engineering Scotland, his employees almost falling over themselves to be helpful, although Lydia noticed that one or two of the younger females seemed to have more than work on their minds if their furtive, hungry glances were anything to go by. Several frankly envious and one or two downright hostile pairs of eyes had met hers through the course of the afternoon, although Wolf seemed totally unaware of the admiration coming his way, his whole concentration fixed on the job in hand. He had sent Doug, and the remnants of his staff who were still around, home just before seven with his customary authority, sweeping aside their offers to stay still later and ordering a management meeting for eight o'clock the next morning.

At half-past seven he threw a sheaf of papers he had been reading on to his desk and stretched noisily. 'Right, that's it for tonight. Food, I think?'

'Is there a chance I could wash and change first?' Lydia asked carefully.

'Yes, there's a chance you could wash and change first,' he mimicked mockingly, his deep voice taking on her wary, careful tone. 'You don't have to tread on eggshells, Lydia, despite the circumstances. I'm a big boy now. I can take adversity in my stride.'

'You couldn't this morning.' She had answered before she had time to think. 'You nearly bit my head off.'

'Ah, well, this morning...' He settled back in his chair, the big powerful body stretching slightly and causing her heartbeat to race a little faster. 'This morning I was still trying to come to terms with the fact that I should have noticed this mess arriving weeks ago.'

'But you couldn't have, no one could——' she began in surprise, only to come to an abrupt halt as he interrupted her, his voice wry.

'I didn't get where I am today without doing just that,' he said slowly, his eyes wandering lazily over her flushed face and the silky tendrils of hair that had worked loose to curl about her face during the course of the afternoon. 'But unfortunately I have had other things on my mind the last few weeks. A distraction,' he added enigmatically.

'Oh, I see.' Elda, no doubt, she thought testily as she wrenched her gaze from his and began to tidy her desk in a corner of the room. Distraction was a novel way of putting it.

'I doubt it.' She didn't look up as he spoke but continued to put the desk in order, switching off the lamp and pushing her chair into place as she stood up. 'I doubt it very much. You really are as innocent as you seem aren't you, Lydia?' he added suddenly.

'What?' Now her gaze did meet his, her eyes wide with shock. She wasn't innocent, there was Hannah——

'I've met sixteen-year-old schoolgirls who were more worldly-wise than you,' he said softly. 'In fact, one or two of my friends have teenage daughters who are worrying them to death. But you... You're just too vulnerable for your own good.'

'Vulnerable?' She reared up as though he had just hit her, and to her it seemed as though he had, at least verbally. He was telling her she was naïve, unable to cope with life, was that it? She stared at him, hurt beyond measure. He thought she was some pathetic creature who was utterly gullible and simple, bare of any sophistication or elegance at all? Not like Elda. Oh, no, she thought painfully. *Definitely* not like Elda. 'I hardly think so,' she said stiffly. 'I do have a daughter, Wolf, and I'm a very good mother.'

'I'm sure you are,' he agreed immediately, 'but that doesn't even touch on what we're talking about. How long did you go out with Matthew before you married him?' he asked abruptly, his eyes searching her flushed face.

'How long?' She stared at him with wide eyes as she struggled to keep the hurt and humiliation from showing. 'It wasn't like that, not with Matthew and me. I'd always known him, you see, we grew up together——'

'But from when you became sexually aware of each other,' he insisted softly. 'How long?'

Sexually aware? she thought faintly as she blushed hotly, her eyes dropping from his. How could she answer that? Had she ever been sexually aware of Matthew? She remembered her wedding-night and their confused fumblings, and the warmth in her cheeks burnt hotter. She hadn't liked that side of married life at first, but Matthew had been gentle and undemanding, and although their lovemaking had been infrequent she hadn't found it disagreeable. But she had never found him sexually attractive. The sudden knowledge was the worst sort of betrayal of his memory, and she closed her eyes tightly against it before she opened them to face Wolf again. She would have to think about this later. It was too much to absorb now with Wolf watching her with those piercingly intuitive eyes.

'We got engaged when I was eighteen and married on my twenty-first birthday,' she said flatly, 'and I don't want to discuss this any more.' She faced him tensely, unaware that the play of emotion across her sensitive, expressive face had intrigued the man in front of her more than he would have thought possible.

He caught himself abruptly. What the hell was he doing asking her personal questions, anyway? He was too old and too wise, far, far too wise, to play with fire.

'Neither do I.' He smiled coolly, a remote, imperturbable expression settling on the hard features that suggested they had been discussing something of no more interest than the weather. 'But I *am* hungry. How about if we make for the hotel, have a wash and brush-up and use their excellent restaurant? Sound good?' he asked lightly.

'It sounds lovely.' She used all her reserves of willpower and smiled with polite enthusiasm.

She'd got some guts. He stared at her for one more moment before rising and collecting both their coats from the coat-stand in the corner of the room. Something had bothered her more than a little, for a few seconds there she had looked devastated, and yet she was handling it with the sort of bravery he suspected was an integral part of the woman. Damn! He closed his mind off with ruthless determination. She was just a female like any other. *Like any other*.

The company car that Wolf was using during his visit ate up the twenty or so miles to the hotel with consummate ease, but Lydia was so tense she wouldn't have noticed if they had been bumping along in an old jalopy. She tried to keep her mind from returning to the conversation with Wolf, but it was no good. She had to face it, she thought suddenly. Had to accept that what she had thought was a perfect marriage hadn't been. I'm sorry, Matthew. She closed her eyes against the darkness outside the windows that reflected the void in her heart. But she *had* loved him, she had. She hugged the thought fiercely to her. He had been so gentle, so kind, protecting her from anything that might harm her... She sat up suddenly as her mind travelled ruthlessly on. More like an older brother. And he had treated her most of the time like a beloved little sister, spoiling her, preventing any contact from the outside world that might disturb her. They had loved each other, genuinely, but... a vital ingredient that she had seen in some other relationships had definitely been missing. Physical attraction, desire, lust, call it what you would. They hadn't had it. She hadn't even had a personal knowledge of that emotion until—until this man seated next to her with the ice-cold eyes and even colder heart had swept into her life. But she was aware of it now. And she wished with all her heart she wasn't. It was making her exactly what he had accused her of being—vulnerable.

'Here we are.' As they drew into a wide, tree-lined drive she saw a blaze of lights in the distance and saw what appeared to be a small castle, complete with turrets and lit with powerful floodlights. 'Our hotel.'

'This is our hotel?' She turned to the hard profile in amazement. 'But it's absolutely beautiful.'

He smiled as he drew the car to a halt in the car-park to one side of the wide stone steps. 'There are plenty of buildings in Scotland like this, but it is impressive, isn't it?' he agreed lazily. 'The food's excellent.'

She stared at him for a spilt second, noting the easy careless smile and cool composure. He had turned her world upside-down, brought things to light he had had no right to reveal, insinuated she was naïve and pathetic among other things and... And he had the nerve to be totally untouched. She hated him. She really hated him. She turned and stared out of the window in despair. She had been a fool to come.

'Don't you like it?' The deep male voice next to her had a note of almost comical amazement.

'What?' She turned to look into his dark face.

'The hotel.' He gestured towards the building as she turned to him. 'You're glaring at it as though it's Wormwood Scrubs,' he added sarcastically, his voice dry.

'I've never seen Wormwood Scrubs, or any other prison for that matter,' she said haughtily. 'And of course I like it. It's absolutely beautiful.' She glared at him angrily.

'Then why the ferocious frown?' he asked wryly.

'Wolf, you have the right to object if I'm not concentrating at work, you even think you have the right to "suggest" how I wear my hair in the office,' she continued coldly, 'but one thing you do not have the right to is my thoughts. They, at least, are all my own and I have no intention of sharing them with you or anyone else.' She stared at him crossly.

'I see.' He settled back a little further in his seat and she waited for the explosion. It didn't come. Instead he surprised her utterly by reaching forward, after a long moment of studying her angry eyes, and cupping her face between his large hands. 'You have to be the most beautiful lady I have met in my life,' he said quietly, 'as well as the most enchanting. Look at the sky.'

'The sky?' She was beginning to feel she was caught up in one of those awful plays that appeared now and again on television with no beginning and no end and utter confusion all the way through. 'What——?'

'Wait.' He had left his seat and walked round to her door before she could move, helping her out of the car and then slipping his arm round her waist as he turned her head upwards towards the black, velvety sky overhead. The night was icy-cold, with the smell of frost in the clear dry air, and the dark blanket overhead was pierced with a hundred tiny twinkling stars in which the clear orb of the moon sat in silent splendour as it surveyed the world beneath. 'The sky.' He had pulled her back against him so his body was the length of hers, his chin resting in the pale silk of her hair and his arms holding her securely against his hard frame. She didn't see the sky. Every part of her was vitally aware of the powerful male body behind her, the smell and feel of him sending a million tiny signals to nerve-endings she had never known she possessed. 'Beautiful, isn't it?' he asked softly.

'Yes.' She had begun to tremble, but for the life of her she couldn't control the faint tremors. All she wanted, more than anything else in life, was for him to kiss her. And then he did just that.

'You're cold.' He had noticed the shaking she couldn't hide and turned her round to face him, pulling her hard into him as his mouth took hers in a kiss that curled her toes. His mouth was urgent and hungry as they stood there in the shadowed darkness, the crisp clean air and faint smell of winter adding a poignancy to the moment that stayed with her for a long time afterwards. 'Lydia...' His voice was a groan, almost a tortured sound in the still air, but in the next instant she was free as he moved her from him, his breathing harsh and ragged as he stared down into her face. 'This is ridiculous, you know that, madness...'

She couldn't move, couldn't say anything, although she wanted to. All she *could* do was to stare up into his dark, handsome face and wonder how she was going to get through the rest of her life after she said goodbye to this man. And it was imperative she said goodbye, and soon. This dark force, this overwhelming attraction that drew her to him like a moth to a flame would destroy her peace of mind forever if she wasn't careful. He wanted a brief dalliance, a temporary affair at the most, the sort of game he was used to and enjoyed. And she wanted... She stepped back from him so sharply that she almost fell. She wanted nothing. *Nothing*. She wouldn't let it be any other way. If she wasn't strong now she would regret it the rest of her life.

'Shall we go in?' Her voice was as flat as she could make it, but nevertheless she heard the little tremor in its depths and hoped he didn't.

'In?' He had been staring at her, his eyes hungry on her mouth and his face dark with desire.

'In to the hotel,' she said carefully. 'It's cold out here.' It was true, the air was cold with a biting quality all of its own, but the chill that was emanating from deep inside her was far more wintry than anything Mother Nature could dredge up. He wanted her for one thing and one thing only. He hadn't even tried to pretend otherwise. And she felt vulnerable here, in this bleak, beautiful part of Scotland with its majestic beauty and harsh, untamed mountains. He was too seductive, too powerful, too fascinating...

'Of course.' He instantly slipped back into business mode, his face straightening into its habitual handsome mask that revealed little and his eyes veiled. 'You must be freezing.' She was, but the weather had little to do with it.

He tucked her case under one arm, holding his with the same hand, and took her elbow in his other hand, and she felt the contact like an electric shock. His touch was light, but it burnt through her clothing like fire, each nerve vitally aware of his closeness. Idiot, *idiot*, she cautioned herself as they walked towards the main door,

but it didn't help. He only had to touch her and
turned to jelly. So she had to make sure he touched h
as little as possible. It was up to her. But it was going
to be hard. She glanced at his cold, handsome face from
under her eyelashes. Very hard.

CHAPTER SIX

THE interior of the hotel was even more impressive than the outside, and as they entered the sumptuous lobby a bellboy moved forward instantly to relieve Wolf of the suitcases at the same moment as the receptionist glanced up from her desk, the practised, cool smile warming considerably as her eyes fastened on Wolf's tall frame.

'Mr Strade.' The smile warmed to gas mark nine. 'We've been expecting you, sir. Your usual suite is ready.'

'Good.' Wolf's smile was polite but not particularly enthusiastic, but it didn't seem to cool the girl's interest an iota, if the bright gleam in her eyes was anything to go by.

'Would you prefer dinner upstairs, sir, or in the restaurant?' The receptionist's hard blue eyes flicked over Lydia briefly. 'Your usual table has been reserved in case you chose to dine there.' She smiled up at him warmly.

'The restaurant, I think.' He turned to Lydia with dark eyebrows raised. 'Would you prefer to eat there?'

'I...' She pulled herself together with considerable effort as her mind raced. What was this about a suite? And where was her room? And she definitely *would* prefer to eat in the restaurant, surrounded by plenty of other people. 'The restaurant.' She smiled with her mouth as her eyes narrowed. He didn't think she was sharing... Of course he didn't. He couldn't. Could he?

He could. 'Come along.' As the bellboy took the key and picked up the suitcases again, Wolf led her towards the lift.

'Where's my key?'

'What?'

She came to a halt just outside the lift and, as Wolf saw the expression on her face, he indicated for the bellboy to go ahead. 'We'll be up in a moment.'

As the lift doors closed on the young man's studiously blank face, Lydia glared up at Wolf, her eyes darkening to coal-black ebony. 'My key. Where is it?' she asked tightly.

'You don't need a key.' His voice was completely expressionless. 'I have the key to the suite of which your room is one of two bedrooms.'

'You've reserved a suite?' She was trying to keep her voice low, but anger was throbbing through every word and she was fighting a losing battle. 'A suite?' she repeated furiously.

'Yes, Lydia, a suite.' His tone was infinitely patient now, his manner that of a responsible adult dealing with a difficult and troublesome child, which in the circumstances was calculatedly insulting. She glared at him angrily.

'Well, you can just unreserve it,' she said tightly. 'I want my own room.'

'You've got your own room.' His eyes narrowed on her flushed face. 'In the suite.'

'There is no way I'm staying here in a suite with you,' she said tensely. 'I want my own room with my own key.'

'Dammit, Lydia!' The cool control was slipping, she noticed interestedly as he took her arm and roughly pulled her out of the way of an elderly couple who had come to stand just behind them, patiently waiting for the lift, the woman's face bright with interest as she caught the last part of their exchange. 'What the hell do you expect me to do, leap on you in the middle of the night?' he asked curtly.

'I want my own room,' she repeated resolutely. 'I never dreamt——'

'For crying out loud, woman...' He shut his eyes briefly and then glared at her in exasperation. 'I always have the suite when I stay here, and knowing that it had two bedrooms I obviously assumed——'

'I know what you *assumed*,' she said tightly.

'I don't believe I'm having this conversation.' He appeared, for once, completely out of his depth, and then as the lift doors opened she felt a gentle tap on her shoulder.

'Excuse me, dear.' The little old lady was standing behind her, her husband watching anxiously from inside the lift as she reached forward and murmured conspiratorially in Lydia's ear in a stage whisper that was clearly audible to Wolf, 'You stick to your guns, my dear. There is too much of this free love these days—— '

'Right. That's it.' As Wolf took Lydia's arm and marched her the few feet into the lift, the woman's husband made a swift exit to join his wife, taking her arm and walking swiftly in the opposite direction. 'You are going to come up with me, inspect this damn suite and then see you've got nothing to worry about,' Wolf said furiously as the lift took them effortlessly upwards. 'Dammit all, Lydia, every other woman of my acquaintance would be mad if I *hadn't* booked a suite——'

'I'm fully aware of that,' she said icily as she forced herself not to wilt under his temper. 'And I am not "every other woman".' The phrase had cut through her heart like a knife.

'Tell me about it.' He shook his head slightly as leant against the side of the lift and watched her wit. eyes that softened suddenly as they ran over her flushed stiff face and tremulous mouth. 'I haven't been in such a crazy situation since I was eighteen and out on a date in my first car when I really *did* run out of petrol. I seem to remember there was an interfering old busybody about then too, in the first car that came by. My girlfriend disappeared with her and that was the end of that.' He eyed her mockingly as she glanced at him once quickly before fixing her gaze somewhere over his left shoulder. 'I'm really not some sort of sex-crazed animal, you know,' he drawled slowly as the lift drew smoothly to a halt. 'I don't know what impression you've picked up or what little stories or gossip you've been listening to, but I'm not completely without sensitivity.'

'Just morals.' She didn't know what made her say it, perhaps it was the easy mockery in his voice and face when she was as tense as a coiled spring, but once out the words couldn't be retrieved and she stared at him aghast as the handsome face hardened into stone-cold granite and his eyes took on the texture of polished glass.

'I'm going to do us both a favour and pretend I didn't hear that.' She found herself ignominiously frog-marched out of the lift into a small corridor before she could protest. The bellboy had opened the door and placed their suitcases inside and at their approach he prepared to leave, pocketing the folded note that Wolf slipped him with a beaming smile which faded somewhat as he glanced at their grim faces.

'I'm sorry, Wolf.' As soon as the door had closed she launched into an apology before she lost her nerve. 'That was a rotten thing to say and without foundation. I don't know anything about you——'

No, you don't.' His face had relaxed at her words but now he walked across to the drinks cabinet in the far corner of the beautiful lounge, gesturing for her to be seated on the massive corner unit that wound round a large open fireplace in which several logs crackled. 'What would you like to drink?' he asked coolly.

'I don't——' She stopped abruptly. She didn't really drink, Matthew had never approved of alcohol and she wasn't keen on the taste, but she needed something to relax her a little if she was going to get through the rest of the evening without shattering into a hundred tiny pieces. 'Sherry, please,' she answered stiffly.

He poured himself a stiff whisky and brought both glasses over to the settee where she was perched nervously. 'Come here.' He placed the drinks on the coffee-table and took her hand, drawing her up and across the room to a door at the far end. 'This would be your room. It has its own ensuite bathroom, so you needn't emerge until you are fully dressed, with your coat on if you wish.' He eyed her wickedly as she blushed a deep scarlet. The room was huge and very luxurious in soft shades of gold and red, an open door in one wall revealing a magnificent bathroom complete with sunken bath and the biggest shower cabinet she had ever seen. 'There is another bedroom for me, again with bathroom,' he continued blandly as he gestured for her to precede him out of the room, 'and you will notice you can lock your door from the inside. I could perhaps arrange for a bolt to be fitted if you're a little nervous?'

'I'm sure that won't be necessary,' she said tightly as she walked back over to the fire with burning cheeks. He was loving this, just loving it, but then she had made the most colossal fool of herself. Why, oh, why hadn't she waited and made sure of the facts before launching

in with the veiled accusations? But he had just see.
so sure of himself, so in control, as though he had do.
this a thousand times before. And he probably had. She
glanced at him now as he sat down beside her and
reached for his drink. With a thousand different women.
Her heart pounded violently. And that was what had
made her so mad. The self-knowledge was a bitter pill
to swallow.

'I'll carry your suitcase through in a moment and you
can freshen up a little before we go down to dinner.' He
glanced at her now and she felt her pulse leap at his
closeness. She could cope with him in an office situation, just, but this was too informal, too intimate. 'That
is, if you're staying?' he added softly, with one raised
eyebrow.

'Of course I'm staying.' She reached for her glass with
a jerky hand and swallowed half the sherry in one gulp.
She would have liked to edge down the settee a little but
didn't dare. The evening was enough of a disaster as it
was without adding to her crimes. 'I misread the situation before,' she added, as coolly as she could.

'That you did,' he agreed gravely, but with an underlying throb of amusement in his voice that added to the
heat in her cheeks. She swallowed the rest of the sherry
without even realising what she was doing, and he took
the empty glass and silently refilled it, sitting down next
to her again with a little sigh. 'It's been a hell of a day,
hasn't it?' He stretched out his long legs as he spoke and
she nodded a reply as she watched him through her
lashes. He had leant back against the settee, closing his
eyes, the glass of whisky held loosely in one hand, and
she couldn't believe what the casual pose was doing to
her hormones, the ones she hadn't known she had until
recently. He had to be the most sexy, flagrantly mas-

...ne, attractive man she had ever met in her
...nole——

'Would you like to phone and see how Hannah is?'

She jumped so violently as he spoke that the rest of
her sherry, which fortunately wasn't much as she had
been sipping it unknowingly as she watched him, disappeared down the front of her blouse. Hannah. She
felt a moment's deep and piercing guilt. Here she was,
sitting positively ogling this man, lusting after him, and
she hadn't given her daughter a thought. 'Yes, yes I
would. Where...?'

'Over there.' He gestured to the phone with one hand
as his eyes narrowed on her flustered face. 'And relax,
Lydia. This is supposed to be the time of the day when
you *relax*,' he added grimly, frowning slightly.

She spared him a cool smile as she rose hastily and
walked across to the phone. If he'd read her thoughts...
She felt her heart leap against her ribcage. But he
couldn't. Thank goodness. A fragile defence but better
than nothing.

Hannah was fine, and after a brief conversation with
her mother she turned to face Wolf again with a composure that was hard-won. 'I'll just change...' She indicated her stained blouse and he rose immediately,
carrying her case into her room without speaking and
leaving quietly, closing the door behind him.

She sank down on one of the large twin beds once she
was alone, and willed her racing thoughts to slow down.
She had to pull herself together: this just wouldn't do.
She was acting like a teenager on her first date, for
goodness' sake. She lay back on the soft cover for a
moment and shut her eyes. But then, this was probably
how people *did* feel on a date—she wouldn't know,
would she? There had only ever been Matthew, after all,

and he had always been as familiar as her own skin.
sat up abruptly and shook her head at her though.
Anyway, this *wasn't* a date, first or otherwise. She was
going to have dinner with her boss on what was a brief
business trip, and that was that. She reached for her case
and began to unpack quickly. But that kiss... She made
an exclamation of annoyance at herself out loud. That
kiss had happened because he was trying it on to see
how she would respond. It was as simple as that. She
might be unworldly in his eyes, vulnerable even, but even
she knew that most men were capable of sleeping with
a woman without it meaning a thing. And he had already
admitted that emotional ties, even the vaguest sort of
involvement, were not his style. She bit her lip hard. He
probably thought that if she had recently separated she
would be missing that particular...ingredient of married
life. Even that he would be doing her a favour? She
reared up at the thought, and stalked into the bathroom
as though Wolf himself had voiced it.

When she emerged from her room some fifteen
minutes later Wolf was waiting for her, his eyes lazy as
they wandered over the smart but feminine soft wool
dress in pale cream, and ultra-slender high-heeled shoes
in the same shade. She had chosen the outfit because
the dress gave her poise and confidence and the shoes
an extra two inches in height. She had the feeling she
would need all the help she could get tonight. One look
at his dark face confirmed the thought.

'You look beautiful, Lydia,' he said softly, 'but
perhaps a more casual hairstyle?' he suggested blandly.

She touched the tight knot at the back of her head
that she had purposely strained every last hair into, and
smiled brightly, her eyes expressionless. 'I don't think
so.' She fiddled with the clasp of her bag so that she

...ld let her eyes drop from his—that clear blue gaze
...as a little disconcerting. 'This is a working trip, after
all.'

'Of course.' There was something in his voice she
couldn't quite place, but when she glanced at him quickly
the hard, male face was cool and cynical, his eyes
hooded. 'Ever the perfect secretary. But you do allow
yourself to eat, I trust?' He moved across and opened
the door into the corridor, waving her through with a
mocking flourish. As she passed she felt his hand on the
clasp at the back of her head but was too late to do
anything about it as her hair swung in a soft silky veil
to frame her face and shoulders. 'That's better.' There
was immense satisfaction in the arrogant male voice as
he glanced down into her angry eyes. 'Far more
comfortable,' he added lazily.

'I thought you insisted that your employees dressed
and behaved discreetly?' she said tightly, as the words
he had spoken that day weeks ago came back to her.

'I have nothing at all against your being discreet,
Lydia.' He smiled slowly. 'Far from it.' She glared at
him in reply and the smile deepened. 'But surely you
understand part of being a good secretary is to keep your
boss happy?' It was such an outrageous line that she
couldn't formulate an adequately scathing rejoinder
before the lift glided upwards and the doors opened, but
as she walked past him, head held high, her eyes flashed
fire.

The dining-room appeared full as they entered, the
tables all at a discreet distance from each other, with
subdued lighting and beautiful furnishings adding to the
general air of unashamed opulence. A waiter appeared
as though by magic at Wolf's shoulder and seemed to
know instantly who he was, ushering them both to a

perfectly positioned table for two in an elegant alcove where they could see everything but remain relatively unobserved themselves.

'Could you bring us a bottle of my usual champagne?' As the waiter handed them two large, heavily embossed menus he nodded immediately, his face deferential.

'There's one on ice now, Mr Strade,' he said quietly.

Lydia saw him raise his hand to someone just outside her line of vision and within seconds an ice-bucket complete with vintage Bollinger was placed in front of them. She might have known. An expression of distaste flickered across her face for a brief moment. Was he treated with this ingratiating respect that bordered on reverence *everywhere* he went? No wonder the man's ego was jumbo-sized. She glanced up to find the vivid blue eyes tight on her face, their depths intuitive. 'Don't frown,' he said drily.

She opened her mouth to protest that she wasn't, but then realised she was and shut it again abruptly.

'And I can't help it if money talks, it's the way of the world.' The hard gaze moved over her pink cheeks slowly. 'With most people, that is . . . Now, what would you like to eat?' he asked smoothly.

She glanced at the menu apprehensively. Was it going to be one of those ultra-sophisticated non-readable items in French? There were several languages, but thankfully English was one of them, and she was able to select the first and main course without any difficulty, which Wolf duly relayed to the waiter once he returned after a discreet interval. As he did so she glanced carefully round the room. It must cost a king's fortune to eat in a place like this if the clientele were anything to go by.

'How was Hannah?'

Her eyes snapped back to his and she saw he was surveying her thoughtfully, his gaze narrowed.

'Fine, thank you, she's very adaptable,' she said carefully.

'She seemed a plucky, sensible little kid on the night of the accident,' he agreed quietly. 'You must love her very much.'

'Yes, I do.' She smiled warmly as she pictured her daughter's bright little face. 'You were very good with her that night, Wolf, especially for a confirmed bachelor,' she finished lightly, and then was suddenly conscious as she looked into his face that a mask of ice had frozen over the hard features.

'My daughter was the same age when she was killed.' The words hung in the air, stark and raw, and for a moment Lydia stared at him helplessly, her mouth half-open.

'Wolf——'

'It was a long time ago, Lydia, buried in the past now.' It didn't look as though it was buried, she thought with stunned horror as her wide eyes took in his taut mouth and haunted eyes. 'My wife and daughter were involved in a car accident eight years ago and both killed instantly,' he continued expressionlessly, his voice flat. 'From that point on it seemed . . . logical to concentrate on my work and keep emotional strings to the minimum.'

'I didn't know . . .' She tried to think of something comforting to say, something uplifting, but her mind was completely blank with the shock of what she had just heard. His wife was dead and they'd had a child? *A child*?

'There is no reason why you should.' He poured them both a glass of champagne as he spoke, his movements perfectly controlled and calm although Lydia knew, somehow, that despite appearances he wasn't feeling like that inside. 'As I said, it was a long time ago.' He smiled, but it didn't reach the beautiful blue eyes. 'Life goes on.'

'I'm so sorry, Wolf.' Her eyes were luminous with unshed tears; she actually felt the pain he must have suffered, and as he gazed into her white face he was completely still for a moment before gesturing abruptly, his voice suddenly harsh.

'No need.' He picked up her glass and placed it in her hand, his face suddenly closed and cold. 'Have a sip of champagne, it's rather good.'

She drank automatically, the clean, cold, sparkling liquid barely registering on her senses as she struggled to absorb the enormity of what he had told her, and when she put down her glass she was surprised to find it was empty and that her head felt a little muzzy. Two glasses of sherry and now champagne on an empty stomach, she thought suddenly. She really mustn't drink another thing tonight.

Wolf's revelation seemed to have robbed her mind of any normal conversation. She wanted to ask him a hundred questions, not one of which was possible, and to follow with light chit-chat after such a disclosure would have been the height of callous insensitivity. She stared at him now as she searched for something, anything, to say. He was sitting in apparent easy contemplation of his fellow diners, big body relaxed and lazy and his gaze indolent as it flicked round the massive, dimly lit room. He seemed at ease with himself and the world in general, but Lydia was beginning to understand that outward appearances were subtly misleading with this man. What went on behind that closed, shuttered mind was his business and his alone. He let very little of himself be seen. It was unnerving, to say the least.

'I shouldn't have told you,' he said suddenly.

'What?' As the blue eyes fastened on her face she hadn't had time to school her expression into what he would want to see.

'About Carrie and my wife—I shouldn't have told you.' He shook his head slowly as he looked into the dark depths of her eyes. 'It's upset you and now you feel sorry for me. Is that about right?' he asked grimly.

She was aware she had to answer carefully, very carefully, if he wasn't to clam up for good. 'I'm sorry that someone as young as Hannah didn't have the chance to grow up,' she said slowly, 'very sorry. I think if I feel grief for anyone it's for her.' She mustn't show him pity, he would abhor it, but it was hard when every soft female instinct in her body wanted to comfort and reassure.

He held her gaze for a long, considering moment before sighing softly as he leant back in his seat, his face suddenly open again. 'That's exactly what tormented me,' he said quietly, his eyes looking inward to something only he could see. 'She had the whole of her life before her.'

'Perhaps she's spending it in a better place.' His eyes moved to focus on her again, their sapphire light piercing.

'Do you believe that?' he asked quietly.

'Yes.' She returned his look bravely, without wavering. 'In the case of children, I do believe it.'

'I'd like to.' His voice held unutterable sadness.

As the waiter appeared at their side with the first course, the shutter came down again and she realised the brief moment of intimacy was over. As she ate the best prawn cocktail she had ever tasted in her life she realised they hadn't discussed his wife at all, and yet he must have been devastated at her death too. How long had they been married? What was her name? What had she looked like? A thousand little questions buzzed at her mind but she resolutely forced them into her subconscious.

At some time in the last few minutes Wolf had refilled her glass and again she took a sip almost automatically. He was such an enigma, this man. How could anyone, anyone at all, walk a solitary path through life? It was...unnatural.

The trout, when it arrived, was excellent, served with baby new potatoes and a selection of vegetables that positively melted in the mouth but, delicious as the food was, Lydia found she was eating almost mechanically. The picture she had had of Wolf in her mind, the picture *he* had deliberately painted for her and everyone else, didn't fit with this new side to him and it unnerved her.

She glanced across the table at him now and found he was watching her, his blue eyes piercingly fixed on her face. 'Are you enjoying the meal?' He smiled lazily, but the sapphire depths shaded by their thick black lashes didn't flicker. 'It's Scottish trout, of course.'

'It's wonderful.' She smiled back carefully, her mind anywhere but on the food. 'But I suppose you're used to eating like this all the time.'

'Is that what you suppose?' His voice wasn't un-friendly but definitely dry. 'You see me as a high-flying socialite, is that it?'

'No——' She stopped abruptly as she saw the glimmer of amusement in the dark face watching hers. 'Not exactly,' she finished weakly.

'I have a house in London close to Hyde Park, with a garden that persists in rebelling against all efforts to control it,' he said quietly, his eyes slumberous now as they stroked over her pale skin. 'My housekeeper lives in . . . with her husband,' he added wickedly, as though she had voiced the suspicion that immediately sprang most unfairly to life. 'The house is an indulgence for a man living alone, but I loathe flats and, contrary to your suppositions, I much prefer eating at home, although I have to admit I rarely get the chance. I have two dogs and two cats inherited from my married years, all of which are geriatrics with enough idiosyncrasies to fill a book. Anything else you'd like to know?' he added blandly.

'I wasn't prying,' she objected indignantly as hot colour flooded her face.

'Weren't you?' He eyed her lazily. 'How disappointing.'

She stared at him without speaking, for the simple reason that she couldn't think of a word to say.

'I have a house in Madeira where I try to escape for at least a month every summer to recharge my batteries,' he continued in the same quiet voice, 'although unfortunately it does have a telephone which I am seriously thinking of having taken out. Last year was a series of interruptions. Every time I stretched out by the pool to take in a few rays, the damn thing went crazy.'

'Oh . . .' The thought of him barely clothed made her hot. And weak. Definitely, deliciously weak.

'And that's about it in a nutshell.' He spread his hands wide and leant back in his chair as the waiter came to remove their plates. 'Any surprises?' he asked expressionlessly.

'Not really.' She was lying. She had seen him in a smart bachelor flat that was elegant and impersonal and never, never in her wildest dreams had she imagined him bothering with any pets. 'What are the animals' names?'

'The dogs are retrievers, Honey and Muffin, and the cats are Meenie and Mo. So there you are, you know it all now.' He smiled dismissively. 'And how about dessert? The strawberry pancakes are especially good.'

'Lovely, thank you.' The change of subject was sudden and intentional and it hurt. His face was guarded now, his eyes hooded, and she sensed he regretted the brief intimacy had happened. She was just a ship that had passed, or was passing, in the night. She mustn't forget that.

The rest of the evening passed in a haze of good food and light conversation, with Wolf acting as the perfect dinner companion, and although she knew it was an act, that he had deliberately set out to charm and entertain her on a superficial level, nevertheless she found she was enjoying herself immensely. He was devastatingly witty and unashamedly wicked, his sense of humour in perfect tune with hers. They sat for some time over coffee and brandy, the latter accepted by her without a qualm as the soft, rosy glow of the evening lowered all her defences, and it was with a real sense of loss that the realisation the evening had finished washed over her. She couldn't remember enjoying herself more.

'Would you like more coffee in our suite?' Wolf asked quietly as he moved back her chair and took her arm as they left the restaurant, his hand firm and warm on her flesh.

'Oh, no, thank you, I shall never get to sleep as it is,' she answered dreamily, her face upraised to his as she replied, and her hair silky-soft and pale as it framed her flushed skin and sparkling eyes.

'I have a perfect remedy for sleeplessness.' The deep voice was faintly mocking and definitely sensual, and as she met the narrowed eyes in which a small blue flame flickered her heart began to pound with a mixture of excitement and nervous anticipation.

She wanted to sleep with him. The thought was both shocking and intoxicating. She remembered the embraces she had shared with Matthew in those years that seemed so long ago, the lukewarm intimacy and careful, gentle familiarity that had nevertheless produced Hannah, and imagined what lovemaking with Wolf would mean. The blood ran through her veins like liquid fire and she felt a tightness in her lower stomach that caused her to stumble slightly. The hard hand on her arm checked the movement instantly and he drew her protectively into his side as they entered the lift, his body supportive.

'I forgot you don't drink.' His eyes smiled down at her but his mouth was sensual, and his lips lightly stroked her forehead as he folded her into his arms in the seclusion of the snug little box. 'Do you still love him Lydia?' She froze as his voice murmured the words in her ear, but he moved her slightly from him so he could see her face and she saw his eyes were determined. 'Do you?'

'Not in the way you mean.' It was the truth, and carried an unmistakable genuineness, but his mouth still tightened at her reply.

'What the hell am I supposed to read into that?' he asked grimly, and then as she opened her mouth to tell him the whole of it, that she had been without Matthew for three years, that she was a widow, he put his finger on her lips and pulled her roughly against him again. 'No, don't answer that. I'd rather not know.'

'But, Wolf——'

'I said no.' As he took her mouth it was almost as though there was pain in his desire, his lips hard against hers, savage even, but then, as the lift drew smoothly to a halt and the doors opened, he lifted his head and scooped her into his arms, carrying her across the few feet of corridor and setting her down with one arm tightly round her waist as he unlocked the door.

'Wolf——'

'No—don't talk, don't think. For once just do what you want to do.' He drew her inside and immediately kissed her again, his hands running over her back in a soft feathery caress that brought a million nerve-endings into glorious life. 'And you want to make love with me, don't you?' He touched her aching breasts lightly. 'Don't you, Lydia?' he persisted softly.

'I can't——'

'Yes, you can.' As his hands shaped the fullness of her breasts through the soft material of the wool dress she felt flames of fire wherever he touched, her arousal immediate. She couldn't believe the way her body reacted to his; nothing in life so far had prepared her for the onslaught of fierce physical desire that coursed through her small frame, leaving her trembling and shaking in his arms.

He began to explore her mouth with experienced, teasing caresses, his lips and tongue first soft and light, then hard and thrusting until she felt a heat rising inside her that had to have release. His mouth wandered to her ears, her throat, finding secret erotic places that had her moaning in his arms as the warmth of his lips worked a magic she found it impossible to resist. He was good, much, much too good at this.

She found she was clinging to his hard-muscled shoulders as much for support as the pleasure of having his powerful body beneath her hands, the smell and taste of him all-encompassing. And he was making no attempt to hide his reaction to their lovemaking, his desire urgent and unashamed and his arousal obvious as he moulded her into the length of his lean, muscled body. There was something breathtakingly satisfying in knowing that she could make this tough, fascinatingly masculine man want her so badly. The knowledge was dangerously erotic, heady.

'I need you, Lydia. I'm sleeping, eating, living you...' His breath was warm and clean against her throat as he covered her skin in tiny, passionate kisses in between each word. 'It's driving me crazy.' She melted against him, unable to stand any longer, and as he lowered her gently on to the thick carpet she felt his hands slide up the satin-smooth skin of her legs. 'I want you and you want me; it's as simple as that.'

As simple as that? She twisted under him, moving to the side and then away as she scrambled to her feet, her heart pounding. Simple, like with all those other women? A sating of bodily need, a physical release? What was she doing? *What was she doing?*

'No.' She stared at him, her eyes huge pools of tortured darkness in the pale delicacy of her face, her lips trembling. 'I can't...'

'Lydia——' As he took a step towards her, his body as taut as a rod and his face working with a hundred different emotions, she backed from him desperately, her hand to her mouth. He stopped instantly. 'Don't look like that, I'm not going to hurt you,' he said furiously, his eyes bleak.

Hurt her? She felt a moment's hysteria before she brought it sharply under control. He had the power to destroy her, never mind hurt her. 'Leave me alone.' She backed from him across the room. 'I can't be what you want me to be, I can't just...' She waved her hand fe-

verishly in the air. 'It has to mean something. I'm sor
She felt the handle of her door beneath her fingers ar
turned to stumble through, her eyes streaming with tears,
blind and deaf to everything but her own humiliation,
shame and misery. How could she have come so close
to betraying herself like that? So close to sleeping with
him when she knew it would mean less than nothing to
him, merely another in the long line of temporary di-
versions, a physical sating of the senses that would be
forgotten as soon as the bodily need was eased. He had
told her what he wanted in his relationships, he had
spelled it out loud and clear. She had no excuses, none
at all.

As the door closed behind her Wolf stood exactly
where she had left him, his mouth a white slash in the
hard line of his jaw. 'It has to mean something.' He drove
his clenched fist against the palm of his hand, his face
savage. And it clearly wouldn't with him. And why? Because she still loved that damn fool who had walked out
on her, on her and the young child who was Lydia in
miniature. This had to be the ultimate irony in his life
so far. But now he knew exactly where he stood. He
strode across the room and poured himself another half-
tumbler of whisky, taking the bottle with him as he
walked into his bedroom and shutting the door with a
savage kick.

CHAPTER SEVEN

WHEN Lydia awoke the next morning it was to heavy, driving rain against the bedroom window, and as she glanced at her tiny travel alarm the illuminated dial told her it was half-past five. That meant she had had precisely three hours' sleep after hours of heart-searching following the disastrous confrontation with Wolf. Her heart thudded as she remembered the whole catastrophic finish to the evening in its entirety. It was all very well to blame the alcohol, the seductive surroundings, even him, but... She shook her head slowly as she climbed wearily out of bed and padded across to the bathroom. She'd wanted him to make love to her and then she had chickened out. He must think she was the worst sort of tease. The tears started again and she brushed them aside angrily. Useless to say that she hadn't been thinking straight, that for once in her life she had gone with her feelings and not her head. She'd made a hopeless mess of the whole thing and she wouldn't blame him if he packed her straight back to London this morning. And how was she going to face him, anyway? She shut her eyes tightly as she let the warm, cleansing flow of the shower ease away some of the aches of a restless night. She could just imagine the cool mockery and veiled contempt with which he would meet her this morning.

When she did meet him at seven o'clock, for breakfast served in their suite, his face was completely expressionless. 'Good morning.' He nodded to her as she

left her room, face burning and head held high. She
wanted to sink through the carpet but forced herself to
join him at the small dining-table to one side of the full-
length window. 'The waiter has just brought the food
up.' He indicated the beautifully laid out breakfast complete with a small posy of yellow and white daisies in
the centre of the table. 'Would you like to help yourself?'
he asked flatly.

'Thank you.' If she ate anything it would choke her,
she thought painfully, but then as she saw his full plate
and the way he seemed to be eating with every appearance of enjoyment, a perverse pride made her select
a more than adequate meal. Each mouthful was an en-
durance test but she managed to clear her plate. It didn't
help that the whole meal was eaten in absolute silence,
Wolf remote and sombre behind his newspaper. But she
hadn't met the cool and cynical mockery she had expected. She glanced up now as she finished her coffee.
She didn't understand him at all. Suddenly the newspaper lowered and a pair of very blue and very clear eyes
met hers. 'It's going to be a hard day,' he said slowly,
'and a long one.'

'Yes, I suppose it is,' she agreed quietly.

'So the first thing I would like to do is apologise for
last night.' As she opened her mouth to speak he raised
his hand quickly, his face dark and severe. 'No, hear me
out, Lydia, please. The second is to say it was not my
intention to take advantage of you——'

'I wasn't drunk,' she protested weakly. She hadn't expected him to behave like this: she had expected rage,
contempt, cold mockery——

'I'm aware of that.' He smiled grimly. 'But you aren't
used to alcohol, by your own admission, and you had
drunk enough to feel . . . a little reckless? I misunder-

'tood the situation and thought——' He stopped abruptly and her face flamed still further. She knew *exactly* what he had thought and she couldn't blame him at all. It had been her body giving the 'go' signals there, and she knew it.

'It was my fault, Wolf,' she said bleakly. 'I don't know what came over me.' Liar. *He* had come over her, the little voice in her mind sniped immediately.

'Well, don't let's argue the finer points.' He rose from the table as he spoke and held out his hand, his eyes veiled. 'Suffice to say we both know where we stand and perhaps we could leave it at that? This project we're involved in is important to me, Lydia, damn important, and I don't want any outside difficulties or tension to deflect our concentration.' His voice was expressionless and cold.

'Of course.' She had never felt so miserable in her life, she thought desperately as she smiled brightly and nodded her agreement. She had been right; she wasn't even a serious consideration in his life. He could dismiss her without a second thought as a write-off. She took his outstretched hand as he helped her up from the table, and let go immediately as the warmth of his flesh sent a shiver down her spine. 'I'll just get my things,' she said quickly.

It had stopped raining as they left the hotel and a weak November sun had lit the grey-blue sky with streaks of gold. The hotel was just past a small village, screened by trees and set back from the main road, and as they drove out of the beautifully tended grounds she glanced in the distance to where craggy mountain peaks of red sandstone and granite topped with white quartzite towered over wild hills dotted with grazing sheep.

'It's lovely in the summer.' He had followed her eye to the harsh, haunting beauty of the bare hills. 'A sea of heather colours the fells purple, and the contrasts of shades have to be seen to be believed.'

'I can imagine.' She nodded stiffly. How could he talk so normally, how *could* he? 'But it's beautiful now in its own way,' she said quietly, forcing herself to make conversation.

'Yes, it is.' The big, powerful car drove swiftly past the tiny village of whitewashed houses and carved gravestones in the ancient churchyard, reaching within minutes the main road which was the fastest route to Inverness, where Wolf's factory was situated. Lydia tried to relax on the short journey to the office, but it was difficult with his big, aggressively male body so close to hers and the scent of him teasing her nostrils. In spite of every effort to the contrary, she kept remembering how it had felt to be in his arms last night. It was everything she had imagined and more. She kicked herself mentally, hard. Stop it, Lydia, she told herself sternly, you're being ridiculous. But, ridiculous or not, her body continued to play tricks on her all the way to Strade Engineering Scotland, and she was immeasurably thankful when the Rover drew to a halt in front of the offices. Never had a journey seemed so long.

The day proved every bit as arduous as Wolf had suspected, but by late afternoon the onerous hours of hard labour had paid off. The contract was saved, albeit with a few concessions. 'I didn't think you'd pull it off, Wolf.' Doug Webb ran a weary hand over his face as he spoke, his eyes red-rimmed. Wolf on the other hand looked every bit as fresh and razor-sharp as when he had stridden into the office first thing that morning, barking orders and setting the place scuttling.

'Piece of cake.' Wolf grinned at the other man with sardonically raised eyebrows, and Lydia felt an emotion shoot through her that caused her breath to stop in her throat. Just physical attraction, she told herself sharply as she tidied the last of the papers on her desk. The fact that he had just looked like a proud schoolboy receiving a hard-won accolade had *not* stirred her heart an iota. She did *not* feel tenderness or warmth towards this man, she did not.

'Hell!' Doug suddenly clapped his hand to the side of his head. 'I was supposed to ask you this morning——' He stopped abruptly. 'Sue'll kill me.'

'She will?' If Lydia had been looking she would have seen Wolf's easy expression stiffen somewhat. 'What's wrong?'

'I was to let her know before lunchtime if you couldn't make it for dinner tonight,' Doug admitted shamefacedly. 'You and Lydia, that is. Otherwise she was going to go ahead with a dinner for four. You know how Sue loves entertaining.'

'Yes.' This time a certain inflexion in Wolf's voice caught Lydia's ear and she glanced up to see the habitual expression of cool remoteness had settled over the hard features. 'Well, we were going to enjoy a quiet meal at the hotel, but you'd better ring Sue and let her know what time to expect us,' Wolf said with neutral politeness.

As soon as they drew up at Doug Webb's smart, detached house the door opened, and a tall elegant woman positioned herself in the lighted doorway, arms stretched out in dramatic welcome. 'Wolf, how lovely. And you must be Lydia.' As they reached her side the slim brunette arched pencil-slim eyebrows as she let her wide, green-flecked eyes wander over Wolf's bland face. 'You

look wonderful, Wolf, it's just not fair that men im-
prove with the years, is it...?'

Lydia found her mouth had fallen open as she preceded
Wolf into the house, his hand in the small of her back.
Doug's wife was not at all what she had expected and
seemed very familiar with Wolf for one of his employees' wives. She glanced at the other woman in the
bright artificial light in the hall and felt her heart sink
as she noticed the tall, model-slim figure and expensive
immaculate dress that draped over the beautiful frame
beneath it as though it had been sewn on. Her own skirt
and blouse were fine for the office, smart and prudently
formal, but hopelessly inadequate for an evening out,
besides which, after the sort of day they had been engaged in, she felt sticky and crumpled and drab.

'Do come through.' Sue took her arm as Doug di-
vested them of their coats, and Lydia saw that the lovely
face was expertly made-up, her long thick dark hair arranged in an upswept style that lent emphasis to the
slender long neck and graceful shoulders. 'You must be
absolutely dying for a drink,' she said languidly.

'Lydia doesn't drink.' Wolf's voice cut in behind her
before she could reply, and she felt herself stiffen at the
expressionless tone. Was he being sarcastic, mocking,
after last night, or merely trying to be helpful? She
couldn't see his face, and turned as they entered the
lounge, but the bland cool features were giving nothing
away, his eyes remote and distant as she searched his
face.

'Don't you?' Sue's voice expressed utter amazement,
with a subtle hint of disapproval at her crassness. 'Well,
we've got tonic or bitter lemon or things like that.' She
smiled at Lydia with her mouth as her eyes swept coldly
over her face and figure with exacting thoroughness.

'There's some freshly squeezed orange in the fridge.' Doug indicated for them to be seated as he spoke.

'That would be lovely.' Lydia forced a smile at his cheerful face gratefully.

'Well, you see to that and I'll look after Wolf,' Sue smiled sweetly. 'Whisky on the rocks, as usual?'

'Please.' Wolf didn't return the lovely brunette's smile but Lydia didn't notice; she was trying to absorb and understand the messages her brain was giving her. There was something wrong, something not quite...nice here.

As Wolf seated himself beside her on the beautifully upholstered settee she glanced round the large room warily. Everything was of the very best. Wolf obviously paid his employees well. She noticed a photograph of two snub-nosed, brown-haired children in a corner of the room, and spoke impulsively as Sue handed Wolf his drink. 'What lovely children. How old are they?'

'Geraldine is seven and Geoffrey is eight. They are Doug's children from his first marriage.' The green eyes flicked uninterestedly over the photograph. 'They live with their mother,' she added coldly.

'Oh, I see.' Lydia sought for something to say—the brunette's tone had almost been a snub. 'Do you have any children?' she asked politely, trying to stifle her dislike.

'No.' Hard green eyes met hers. 'I still work now and again, so it's impractical.'

'Sue is a model.' Doug had joined them, handing Lydia her drink with a quick glance at his wife. 'She feels being pregnant would put her out of action too long, besides which, she doesn't really like children. Do you, darling?' It was obviously a sore point, and Lydia felt herself flush at her inadvertent gaffe, but Sue seemed quite unaffected, throwing her husband a cold glance of distaste as she agreed with him.

'No, I don't.' She smiled coolly at Lydia. 'Deadly for the figure.'

As the evening progressed Lydia felt more and more uncomfortable. Apart from the first few moments, the social repartee had been light and amusing; Sue was a sparkling hostess and Doug was droll and humorous, but under the surface polish of well-bred refinement she sensed a whole host of different emotions bubbling and simmering with puzzling ferocity.

Wolf was his normal cool, cynical self, adding the odd bite of mordant humour which Sue in particular seemed to appreciate thoroughly, but then she seemed to appreciate thoroughly everything about Wolf, Lydia thought testily as the brunette made yet another outrageous bid for his attention, the third in as many minutes. It was obvious and embarrassing, and yet Doug seemed quite relaxed, jovial, even.

Suddenly the beautiful brunette's attention turned to Lydia, her eyes as hard as glass as she looked into her face. 'Is that a wedding-ring I see?' She glanced pointedly at Lydia's left hand. 'You're married?'

'Separated.' Wolf had answered before she could speak, his tone infinitely cold.

'Oh, what a shame...' The narrowed blue eyes flickered a moment. Wolf had made it perfectly plain that further questions would be an intrusion, but his hostess chose to ignore the warning. 'Had you been married long?' she asked silkily.

'I got married when I was twenty-one.' This time Lydia forestalled Wolf. The look on his face indicated that his reply wouldn't have been conducive to harmonious relations.

'Any children?' the smooth voice persisted.

'Sue...' Doug spoke quickly, with a meaningful glance at Wolf's dark face.

'A little girl.' Lydia smiled brightly. 'She's three now and absolutely gorgeous.'

'Is she?' It was clear the last thing Sue wanted to talk about was Lydia's child, so for that very reason Lydia detailed Hannah's life from birth to present and the diversion worked as she had thought it would. Immediately Lydia paused for breath Sue launched into a description of her latest modelling assignment with great gusto, and as the other three listened patiently Lydia caught Wolf's eye. He winked, slowly and very sardonically, before turning away. He had recognised the manoeuvre and given her due acclamation. She quickly checked the surge of pleasure she felt. Careful, Lydia, careful, she told herself silently. It doesn't mean a thing.

All in all she felt overwhelming relief when Wolf glanced pointedly at his watch as they finished dinner and made their apologies. 'It's been a long day,' he drawled lazily as Sue pouted in his direction. 'We're all dead on our feet.'

'A quick coffee, then?' Sue smiled beguilingly. 'It's ready and will keep you awake on the drive back to the hotel.'

Wolf raised enquiring eyebrows at Lydia and, much as she would have liked to shake her head and agree they go immediately, she found herself politely acceding to just one cup. It seemed unnecessarily rude not to.

'Come and help me, Lydia,' Sue invited surprisingly. 'Many hands make light work, and all that.'

Once in the huge fitted kitchen, that was the ultimate in elegance, Sue shut the door carefully, her eyes narrowed as she turned to Lydia and indicated the tray and cups and saucers on the work-surface. 'Have you known Wolf long?' She removed the aromatic pot of coffee from its stand and waited while Lydia set the tray.

'Not really.' Lydia felt the hairs on the back of her neck prickle as though in warning of a confrontation, but told herself she was imagining things. 'His secretary is on maternity leave and I'm standing in for her,' she explained quietly.

'Really...?' Sue stood back a pace and surveyed Lydia's blonde beauty through half closed eyes. 'You aren't the normal sort of office girl, are you?' It was meant to insult, and Lydia stared back steadily as she felt herself stiffen in readiness for the attack. Their glances held for a long moment and Sue was the first to look away, a sudden flush of colour flaring across the high cheekbones.

'There has been a steady stream of young hopefuls in Wolf's life since Miranda died,' the hard voice continued nastily as Sue walked across to a cupboard at the far end of the kitchen. 'You know he was married, of course?' she added as she suddenly swung round to face Lydia, eyes narrowed like a beautiful cat about to pounce.

'Of course.' Whatever impulse had made Wolf share the confidence she blessed tenfold. Sue had obviously hoped and expected it would be a shock. 'The accident must have been a shock for everyone,' she said expressionlessly.

'The women absolutely adore him, you know.' Sue clearly wasn't going to be deflected from her chosen form of attack. 'Well, it isn't surprising, is it? He has to be the most gorgeous man in the whole of London.'

'Well, as his secretary, my job is to organise and help as far as I can in the office,' Lydia said calmly, keeping her temper in check with considerable effort. The woman was a monster.

'Oh, of course...' The words were delivered in such a way as to make them a subtle insult. 'His secretary...' Sue turned and extracted some fresh napkins from the well-stocked cupboard, her movements graceful and cool. She really was elegance personified, Lydia thought dispassionately as she watched the regal brunette carefully, and she had never met anyone she liked less.

She waited quietly for the next attack and it wasn't long in coming as Sue walked over to the tray, slinging the napkins carelessly by the side of the expensive bone china.

'I was his wife's best friend, you know.' She had obviously changed the direction of the assault, Lydia thought warily as Sue spoke again. 'We were both models, of course, and quite inseparable when Miranda married Wolf. She was just so beautiful, everyone adored her.'

'Did they?' Lydia prayed for composure as she watched the other woman open a box of after-dinner mints and place them on the tray. She didn't want to hear any of this, but she had the feeling there was no escape.

'He was just so devastated after the accident, I was *so* glad I was around.' Sue turned hard green eyes on Lydia's pale face. 'To help...you know.' She smoothed her dress suggestively.

Oh, she knew all right, Lydia thought painfully as the green eyes narrowed into feline slits in which the meaning was unmistakable. Suddenly a whole host of little incidents that had bothered her all night fell into place. 'I'm sure your friend would have been very grateful,'

Lydia said coolly, with biting scorn. 'Shall I carry the tray through?'

'And we're still such *good* friends.' Sue's face was poisonous with a mixture of dislike and virulent maliciousness. 'Doug got this job on my recommendation,' she added meaningfully.

'Did he?' Lydia had had enough. She took hold of the tray and walked across the room. 'Well, your husband is very good at his job, so I understand, Mrs Webb, and I'm sure he got the position because Wolf knew he could do the job, not because you were available to sleep with the boss.' She flicked open the door-handle with her hip, almost dropping the tray in the process, and stalked into the lounge with her head held high.

The next few minutes were painful in the extreme. Lydia sat in regal silence, sipping her coffee without looking to left or right, aware of Sue's tight-lipped face as she made desultory conversation with the two men, although it was obvious her heart wasn't in it. Wolf's razor-sharp gaze had flashed over Lydia's face more than once, but she was determined not to give him the chance to enquire what was wrong until they were in the car. And then she'd let him have it. Hot and strong. Her lip curled as she thought of the implications of what Sue had revealed. He'd slept with his wife's best friend for nothing more than sexual gratification, that much was obvious, and then secured her husband a post in his firm. It stank. Whatever way you looked at it, it stank. Was he still sleeping with her when he felt like it? Well, he'd said he wanted relationships with no ties, and what better way to ensure that than to have an obedient husband to take charge when he felt he'd had enough? Her eyes flashed over Doug and she saw he was looking at her with a faintly bewildered expression in the blue eyes. It was awful. Poor Doug. A flood of self-righteous anger added to the sense of outrage. Whatever his first wife had been like, she couldn't be worse than Sue.

They left the house shortly afterwards, Sue effusive in her goodbye embrace with Wolf and stiffly rigid with Lydia.

Once in the car Wolf turned to her, his eyes silver in the dim moonlight trickling in through the car window. 'OK, let's have it.' The deep voice was dry but not unfriendly. 'Obviously Sue's got under your skin in some way? She has a knack of offending practically every woman she comes into contact with.' The conciliatory note was the last straw.

'I can't imagine why.' She glared at him angrily, her eyes black with furious rage. 'But apparently that wasn't the case with your wife? I understand the two were great friends.'

They had been travelling along the neat, newly made road that led on to the small private estate in which Doug's house was situated, but now Wolf turned into a bus pull-in, parking the car with cool controlled movements and turning to her once the engine had died.

'Sue knew Miranda, yes,' he said with studied calm, his eyes stroking over her hot cheeks and glittering eyes. 'Great friends is probably a bit strong, but I think they got on OK.'

'And Sue was so comforting after the accident.' She knew she was going to regret this, but somehow, after all that had gone before, it had to come out.

'Was she?' He eyed her grimly. 'I take it that should mean something?'

'Well, it clearly didn't to you.' How could he be so icy cold, so calm?

'Lydia...' He paused and settled himself further into the seat, studying her through narrowed eyes. 'Would you like to tell me exactly what the hell you're talking about?'

'I'm *talking* about sleeping with your wife's best friend and then giving her husband a job to keep her available,' she said scathingly.

'*What*?' The word was a pistol-shot in the close confines of the car but his face had frozen, the lines round his mouth and eyes standing out in startling contrast to the rest of his tanned skin. And as she looked into his face, into the icy blue eyes, she knew she had made a terrible mistake.

'Sue said——'

'I don't care what the hell Sue said,' he snarled softly. 'Surely it didn't take you above one minute to see the sort of woman she is? She's rotten, Lydia, right through. Life has soured her to the point where she is no good to herself or anyone else. She makes Doug's life hell.' He took a deep breath and then spoke more softly, but still with a cold, deadly intensity that frightened her half to death. 'I knew her long before I met Miranda, when she was just seventeen and I was nineteen, and for a time we had some fun together. Then she got on to the model circuit and everything changed. She changed. But we still moved in the same set and when Miranda came along...' He shrugged tightly. 'I guess they had the work in common. She married Doug three years ago when the modelling contracts began to dry up, and when he lost his job eighteen months ago she suggested I give him an interview. *Suggested*. That's all. Doug got the job on his excellent capabilities. He knows that and I know it and, for the record, Sue knows it too,' he added grimly.

'Wolf——'

'Doug is not just an employee, he's a friend,' he growled softly. She shrank back against the cushioned seat and he gave a small, mirthless smile. 'I've never raised a hand in anger to a woman before but you, Lydia, you push me to the limit. Have I cross-questioned you about Mike Wilson? Have I? And I had every right, believe me, but I tried to believe——' He stopped abruptly. 'Oh, to hell with it.'

Mike Wilson? she thought helplessly. What had he got to do anything? What was he thinking about her? 'Wolf, I don't understand——'

'What do you see when you look at me?' He cut into her voice savagely, his face ruthless. 'Some creature from the pit with horns and a forked tail? Do you seriously think I would employ a man, a good, honest man, for the sole purpose of sleeping with his wife when I felt the need? I haven't touched Sue in eighteen years, although for the whole of that time she's made it very clear she was ready and willing, even before Miranda died.' He gave her a last scathing glance of biting disgust and turned the ignition key, his face white.

They drove back to the hotel in absolute silence, and mercifully Lydia was numb with shock. She realised she had played right into Sue's hands. Somehow the tall brunette had sensed the attraction between Wolf and his secretary and had been determined to destroy what she didn't quite understand. And Lydia had believed her, or *tried* to believe her. The thought pierced the numbness as they reached the hotel grounds. She had wanted to believe the worst of Wolf, needed to; it had been protection against this deadly, overwhelming attraction that made her putty in his hands. If she could despise him, work up some disdain and scorn for the man she thought he was, it would have been a defence against her own

feelings for him. Because, although she knew he di
want any lasting commitment with a woman, althoug
she knew his heart, if he had one, was as cold as ice,
everything in her wanted to throw herself at his feet.
And *that* had been what she was fighting, not him.

'Goodnight, Lydia.' He left her immediately they entered the suite, without giving her a chance to say anything, walking into his bedroom and shutting the door
with a dismissive controlled click. She would have pre-
ferred he slam it hard. At least that way it would have
shown he had some feeling about her left. She stood in
the lounge for a few seconds more, her head whirling,
and then went to her own room on leaden feet.

Well, she had what she wanted now. She stared at her
reflection in the full-length mirror, misty through her
tears. He would leave her alone. She had killed even that
strange animal passion he had felt for her. She hugged
herself tightly round the waist, the image in the mirror
blurring still more. So why didn't she feel relieved,
comforted, reassured? Why did she feel as though the
world, her world, had just shattered into a million tiny,
sharp, piercing little pieces?

CHAPTER EIGHT

SURPRISINGLY, when she surfaced from a thick, deep, heavy sleep the next morning, she realised she had slept the night away. A combination of mental and physical exhaustion along with practically no rest the night before had worked like a powerful sleeping-draught in spite of her overwhelming misery. She glanced at the clock and then looked again more sharply. Ten o'clock? It couldn't be saying ten o'clock? She leant closer and heard the steady rhythmic tick. She must have slept through the alarm at half-past six. She turned the small clock upside-down and saw to her dismay she hadn't set it the night before. Damn! She leapt out of bed with her heart pounding. What would Wolf think? Why hadn't he called her, knocked on the door? Where was he?

She hastily pulled her silk dressing-gown over the matching pale blue nightie and felt for her fluffy mules under the bed, catching sight of her ruffled reflection in the mirror as she did so. She looked a mess but she hadn't got time to worry about that now. Was Wolf at the office? She'd have to ring—this was awful.

She wrenched open her door and had taken two or three steps into the lounge before she realised Wolf was sitting at the table in a replay of the previous morning, newspaper open, table full, and a steaming cup of black coffee in front of him. 'Good morning.' The newspaper lowered, and just for an instant she saw surprise at her attire flash across the hard, handsome face before the blank mask settled again. 'The waiter's just left. D wake you?'

'No... Yes... I don't know...' She stared at him a she struggled to compose her racing thoughts. 'I didn't know you were here, it's so late...' She glanced desperately towards the phone. 'I was going to ring you at the office.'

'And now there's no need.' The dark voice was quite expressionless, his whole manner one of cool, reserved control and careful politeness, but she sensed somehow that below the surface it was a different story. The black eyebrows rose a fraction as his blue eyes wandered over her ruffled hair and sleep-flushed face. 'I had a mental picture of what you would look like in the morning and I'm not disappointed.' She stared at him helplessly, quite unable to move, let alone reply, and after a long moment the newspaper was raised again. 'Why don't you sit down and have some coffee now you're out here?' It was obvious and reasonable and she couldn't think of a reason not to, so she walked gingerly across to the table, pulling the belt of the dressing-gown still tighter round her slim waist as she slipped into a vacant chair.

'There's toast and preserves and a variety of cooked dishes under the covers,' the cool voice behind the newspaper said. 'I ordered enough for two in case you joined me.'

'I'm sorry I'm so late,' she said stiffly to the black and white print. 'I forgot to set my alarm——'

'No problem.' The newspaper crackled a bit but still remained in place. 'Relax and enjoy a leisurely breakfast—you earned it yesterday.'

Yesterday? For a moment she thought he was being sarcastic about the dreadful, ill-fated evening, and then reason asserted itself. He was referring to the long day's

.. Of course he was. She brushed a silky strand of .. off her face. Somehow yesterday had narrowed .own to several catastrophic hours as far as she was concerned.

She must look awful. She touched her hair tentatively. No make-up, and she hadn't even brushed her hair before she had raced out here. She shut her eyes for an instant in exasperation at her impulsiveness and then opened them to pour herself a cup of black coffee. She usually had it white but she needed all the undiluted caffeine she could get this morning—that stimulating alkaloid had better work, and fast. To sit here and eat breakfast with him was bad enough, but with him fully dressed and looking as delicious as ever, and her barely decent... She sighed deeply.

'Now what?' As the newspaper lowered her heartbeat increased tenfold. Freshly shaven and with his still-damp hair slicked back he was just too—too much.

'Sorry?' she gazed at him warily, noting the absence of a jacket. The pale grey shirt sat on the big broad shoulders like an advertisement for its brand name, and the carelessly knotted silk tie matched perfectly. It wasn't fair that one man should have so much going for him.

'The big sigh?' He eyed her sardonically. 'I would have thought you'd be starving this morning. Sue's food may be gourmet style but she serves the sort of portions that she and the rest of her model-friends eat. Hardly satisfying or even remotely adequate. Now, stop contemplating the food and eat it instead.' The newspaper was raised again, leaving her staring at it open-mouthed.

She hadn't dreamt that disastrous finish to the evening, had she? It *had* actually happened? She remembered the black rage on his face and the icy fury that had turned the silver-blue eyes into pinpoints of steel, and shivered

suddenly. But this morning he was so...reasonable. Wha
was going on?

'You'll be seeing Hannah later,' the disembodied voice
said after a moment or two. 'We're catching the two-
thirty plane to London.'

'Oh, right,' she responded weakly.

'We could have stayed another day but Doug can see
to the odds and ends now, and there's a previous appointment at five I'd like to keep if I can. Perhaps you'd
take most of the papers back to the office for me?' he
asked quietly.

'Of course.' A previous appointment? There was some
inflexion in his voice, just something, that told her it
wasn't a business appointment. Elda? The beautiful
brunette's name flashed into her mind and she felt the
piece of toast in her mouth turn to cotton wool. Of
course it would be Elda and why shouldn't it be? He
was a free agent, unattached and fancy-free. He could
see exactly who he liked. The pain in her chest deepened. The corrosive scene last night, her awful accusations he could dismiss as unimportant this morning,
because *she* was unimportant. When would she learn?
When would she ever learn?

She finished the slice of toast quickly and stood up,
her voice cool and flat even as she trembled inside. 'I'll
go and have a bath, if that's all right?' she asked quietly.

'Fine.' His eyes had narrowed at her tone but he made
no other comment. 'I'd like to leave here at twelve and
call in the office for a few minutes, OK?'

'I'll be ready.' She walked with as much dignity as she
could muster into her room, and when she joined him
just before twelve she was the epitome of the perfect
secretary—immaculate, cool, with not a hair out of place
and a remote, businesslike expression tightening her

delicate features. Never again would she betray any emotion to this man, *never*. Her back stiffened with conviction. Once back in London she would give a week's notice and then that would be that. She ignored with ruthless determination the jerk her heart gave at the thought.

Doug was waiting for them at the office, a good-natured, warm smile on his face and his manner easy. It only took one glance for Lydia to realise that Sue hadn't told him what had passed between them the night before. Whatever excuse she had made for the obvious tension, it wasn't the real one. How could some men be so blind where the female of the species was concerned? she asked herself in amazement. Sue was the original barracuda, in fact she made the large voracious hunter seem like a sweet little goldfish, but Doug obviously loved her in spite of the fact that she didn't even like his children. Men were different creatures, she thought faintly, aliens... She glanced at Wolf's hard, cold face silently. Definitely aliens. And she had given this particular alien far too much power where she was concerned.

'Well, all's well that ends well?' Doug grinned cheerfully as they finished checking the last of the figures and gave them to his secretary to fax through. 'Next time you come down I hope you can stay longer, Wolf—perhaps we could put you up? I know Sue would like that.'

Lydia glanced sharply at Doug's smiling face to see if there was an edge beneath the apparent goodwill but no, his face expressed nothing but what his words indicated.

'Thanks, Doug.' Wolf's voice was bland and dry in the extreme. 'But it's probably better if I'm independent. I often work until late in the night and I wouldn't want to keep you up.'

'Well, the offer's always open.' The other man seemed totally oblivious to Wolf's cynical glance at Lydia and her burning cheeks.

Once back in the privacy of the car, Wolf eyed Lydia sardonically as he started the engine. 'Trusting soul, isn't he?' The deep voice was bland and cool. 'Unlike some.'

'If that means me, I think you're being most unfair.' She glared at him angrily. 'I've said I'm sorry for misunderstanding things and I am, but surely you can see how things looked from my side? Sue virtually told me——' She stopped abruptly. 'Well, you know what she hinted at,' she finished helplessly.

'And how readily you believed her.' There was a note in his voice she couldn't place. If she hadn't known it was impossible, she would almost have thought it was pain. The journey home was tight with tension, the air electric. Wolf seemed to have disappeared into a world of his own, his face withdrawn and cold and his body taut, but she barely noticed; her whole being was eaten up with misery. She knew she had to leave this man, and fast, but the thought made her sick with pain. It was ridiculous, crazy, but somehow the idea of never seeing him again had got all out of proportion in her mind. She didn't understand it, or herself, but it was a fact.

Once back in London he settled her in a taxi-cab with a pile of papers to drop off at the office. 'I wanted to talk to you today, but the timing was all wrong.' His face was stiff as he surveyed her through the window. 'There's something I need to discuss with you in some depth, something you need to understand, but it can't be rushed.'

'I'm sure tomorrow will do.' She forced herself to smile brightly. 'You mustn't be late for your appointment.'

'No...' He straightened and stood back from the taxi and just for a moment, an insane moment, he seemed vulnerable and strangely alone among the crowds thronging the terminal, his eyes bleak and uncertain as they held hers. She felt herself leaning forward instinctively but then the taxi moved off and the moment was lost. She sank back against the upholstered seat that smelt vaguely of leather and smoke as her heart thudded its beat violently against her chest. She really must be losing her reason. If the taxi hadn't chosen that second to move away she would have made the most colossal fool of herself for the second time in twenty-four hours. What would she have said to him? She didn't know. What she *did* know was that her hand had been moving to reach out to his. She shut her eyes tightly. He would probably have ignored it with that icy-cold disdain he was so good at or, worse, made a cool cynical remark that would have cut her in two. She had to leave him. *No.* She corrected herself firmly. She had to leave Strade Engineering's employ, that was all it meant. That was all it had to mean.

She dropped her suitcase off at home before continuing in the taxi to the office, where she worked furiously until just on five, when she left on the dot. She wasn't normally time-conscious, just the opposite in fact, but the thought of being around when Wolf returned fresh from Elda's arms was too much. OK, so she had been wrong about Sue, she told herself bleakly as the tube carried her swiftly homewards, but Elda still remained. And it was worse, somehow, that Elda was so inoffensive—likeable even. If she had been another Sue, hard and patently selfish, Lydia could have dismissed her as just another jet-setter out for kicks, but Elda was...nice. And Wolf displayed a gentleness with her that seemed to belie his earlier comments on his attitude to his women. But perhaps this appointment had nothing to do with Elda? The hope died as quickly as it was born. Somehow a primitive instinct that was irrefragable told her it had.

Hannah's welcome was ecstatic, and for an hour or so the ache in her heart eased as she played with her daughter before getting tea. The trip had been hectic and not conducive to shopping, but she had found the perfect present in the airport shop, a delicate gold chain with a tiny little engraved locket that she knew Hannah would love. Matthew had bought Lydia a similar, much larger one on her eighteenth birthday, which had always held untold fascination for her daughter, and now Hannah insisted on keeping hers on as they went upstairs for her evening bath. As she soaped the tiny wriggling body, responding to a long, involved story Hannah was telling her about an incident at nursery, the phone began to ring downstairs.

'Oh, Mummeee...' Hannah's pouting lower lip and disappointed face as she made to lift her out of the bath halted her in her tracks. The phone continued relentlessly. What if it was Wolf? Her stomach lurched helplessly. Well, what if it was? She turned back to Hannah with a reassuring smile.

'Five more minutes and that's all.' If it was Wolf, *if*, he could always phone back later, and why would it be him, anyway? She was beginning to get into the realms of fantasy with this thing, she thought testily. All that had happened, the bare unadulterated fact, was that he had been tempted to indulge in a brief convenient affair with his temporary secretary, and when she had refused

had accepted the rebuff with the minimum of emotion.
He was probably quite relieved, her mind ground on
ruthlessly. Once the initial passion had been sated she
would have become the proverbial millstone round his
neck. He knew, and she knew, that she just wasn't his
type. Naïve, inexperienced, unsophisticated? Probably,
she thought grimly. But if there was a choice of re-
maining as she was or becoming like one of the women
he usually enjoyed, she knew she had had no alternative
but to act as she had. To do otherwise would have been
emotional suicide.

She had just settled herself in front of the television
later that evening, Tiger a warm bundle of purring fur
on her lap, when the telephone rang again.

'Lydia?' Ridiculous, stupid, but at the sound of his
deep, silky voice her oxygen-level took a nosedive. 'Is
this a good moment?' the dark voice asked carefully.

'A good moment?' She tried valiantly to pull herself
together and act like a responsible, mature adult.

'I wanted to talk to you.' There was a brief pause, and
just for a moment she felt he was finding this conversation as nerve-racking as she was, but that was crazy.
'I'd prefer it be somewhere private, not the office.' This
time the pause was longer. 'Are you free now if I come
round?'

'But——' She stopped abruptly and took a long, deep
shuddering breath. What did he want to come round
for? The answer registered in every nerve of her body
and scared her half to death. She *wanted* him to come
round, to make love to her...

'Can you give me some idea of what it's about?' she
asked faintly. Did he think that her rage over Sue had
indicated she was jealous? That she wanted him? That
her 'no' had been a subtle come-on? Perhaps he wasn't

used to being refused, and that apparent calm and cold acceptance of her rebuff had merely hidden a ruthless determination to get his own way?

'You know,' he said quietly. 'This attraction between us.'

'Oh.' His very control was intimidating. He was so much in command of every situation, the master of his own emotions and everyone else's. Suddenly she had to ask, and she knew she wouldn't be able to do it if he stood before her in the flesh. 'That appointment to-night?' She shut her eyes tightly. 'Was it with Elda?' she asked bleakly.

'How did you know?' He sounded surprised, nothing more. No guilt. No shame.

How did she know? The pain that shot through her whole being was shattering. She knew because her love for him had sensitised her to every little thing about him. She knew the look on his face when he thought of Elda, the tone of his voice. She knew so many things about him she had never consciously realised before. Because she loved him. The knowledge had been there with her for weeks but she had been too busy fighting it to let it get through to her brain. She loved him in a way she had never loved Matthew. In a way he had told her he was incapable of and didn't want.

'I don't think it would be a good idea for you to come round, Wolf.' There was a small, blank silence and she forced herself to continue. 'Elda wouldn't like it,' she said painfully.

'Elda?' The name was a small explosion. 'What the hell has Elda got to do with it?'

'Not a lot, probably.' Her heart was pounding so hard against her ribcage she was sure he could hear it. 'Let's just say she's an illustration of the case-history.'

'Lydia, I'm sure that this is making sense to one of us, but it sure isn't me.' She heard a deep, indrawn breath and then his voice spoke again more quietly. 'I'm coming round——'

'No!' For a moment she felt a flash of emotion that was close to hatred. 'Perhaps Elda can stand knowing she is just one in a long line of brief liaisons, perhaps she even really wants it that way, I don't know. What I do know is that I have no intention of being her replacement.' This time the silence on the end of the phone was absolute. And then shockingly, unbelievably, the line went dead. He'd hung up on her. She gazed at the inoffensive piece of plastic in her hands for a full minute before replacing the receiver slowly. He hadn't tried to cajole, reassure, bully... He'd just simply hung up on her. The rejection was a stunning slap in the face. He couldn't have made it plainer how little she mattered.

She began to pace the lounge, Tiger staring up at her with wide, disapproving green eyes as she walked to and fro in an agony of bitter pain. Well, what had she expected? she asked herself wildly. Protestations of undying love? A declaration of a change of heart? An announcement that he had discovered she was the one true love of his life and that he was prepared to give up all for her? She laughed bitterly, that sound a cracked, dry exclamation of pain in the quiet room. She *had* harboured such stupidly romantic hopes in the secret recesses of her heart, she admitted to herself grimly, even if she hadn't acknowledged them to herself. And now she had got exactly what she deserved. She clenched her hands together and forced herself to sit down on the settee. He had lost a wife and daughter and his heart had died with them. End of story.

The sharp, angry knocking on her door a few minutes later took no account of a small child sleeping. *He had come to see her.* As she stumbled forwards she wasn't sure if it was anger, pain, relief or wild exhilaration that had turned her legs to water, but as she flung open the door, to reveal Wolf dark and scowling on the doorstep, she knew the main component of her emotion was burning rage. Rage that he could put her through this, rage that she meant so little in comparison to what she felt for him, rage at Elda and the hundred and one others like her——

'Elda is the wife of my best friend.' As she automatically tried to close the door, stunned at the outrageous lie, he thrust his foot in the space and jerked the handle out of her hand. 'Oh, no, you're going to listen, listen to every damn word I want to say.' The words were low and furious and all the more deadly for being spoken in a quiet, controlled hiss. 'I don't know what this husband of yours has done to you to make you so distrustful of the male gender, but I sure as hell intend to find out.' She found herself manhandled back into the lounge and sank down on to the settee as her legs refused to support her another moment.

'Elda is Andrew's wife—the doctor I called out to you when you hurt your head?' She nodded helplessly as he stood in front of her, magnificent and frightening in his black rage. 'I've known them both since university and there has never been a couple more deeply in love,' he continued grimly, his eyes lethal. 'But Elda can't have children, or to be more precise she can't carry a baby more than twelve weeks. It's been miscarriage after miscarriage, I've lost count, and since the last one a year ago she's got it into her head that Andrew is going to leave her for someone else who can give him children.

I know that it's the last thing on Andrew's mind, *he's* nearly been going insane trying to convince her that he loves her more than any desire for procreation, but six months ago she tried to kill herself and things got really heavy for a time. She can talk to me, she trusts me.' He eyed her condemningly as he said the last three words. 'And Andrew and I both thought it was better than a psychiatrist, so I've been there for her—for them both.'

'And the appointment?' she asked through numb lips.

'Elda's going to America,' he stated expressionlessly. 'A colleague of Andrew's suggested a doctor who is unparalleled in his work for childless couples, added to which we all thought the change would do her good. The thing is an obsession now, which she has seen at last. She is a lovely lady and I hated to see her so messed up.' He eyed her grimly. 'That is the truth, Lydia, take it or leave it. Andrew is going to join her out there in a couple of weeks when the initial tests have been completed, but he wanted me to turn up before she left as a surprise. She left on the seven o'clock flight,' he added flatly.

'I see.' Totally inadequate, but she couldn't think, let alone speak. 'I'm sorry,' she said weakly.

'So...' He looked down at her, his eyes hooded. 'Do you believe me? Really believe me?'

'Of course I believe you.' If she had been looking at him she would have seen the hard face soften at her total acceptance of the ignominious position she had placed herself in. 'It was just after all you'd said——' She stopped abruptly. This was her fault. She'd jumped to all sorts of conclusions without any real knowledge of the facts, and she couldn't blame him, not even indirectly. Oh... She bit on her lower lip painfully. What an utter fool she'd made of herself. 'I'm sorry,' she said again, her voice wretched.

'I haven't looked at another woman since the first day I set eyes on you.' The deep softness in his voice brought her head jerking up, her eyes wide as they met his. 'If that helps at all? Not that there was a steady stream before that, I might add.' He smiled slowly. 'Your faith in my prowess in that direction is more than a little touching.'

'Wolf——'

'I need to talk to you, Lydia. I should have done it weeks ago but I wasn't ready, you weren't. I knew you were hurting and I wasn't sure if your marriage was really over. Added to which——' He stopped abruptly. 'Dammit, woman, don't look at me like that, I can't think straight,' he said thickly.

'Wolf...' His name was a plea for understanding.

As he reached for her a little movement behind him caught Lydia's eye. 'Hannah?' Wolf turned in the same instant and they both surveyed the tiny pink and white angel standing in the doorway with sleep-smudged eyes and silky blonde hair, a battered teddy bear tucked under one arm. It was a picture guaranteed to win first place in anyone's affections, and as Lydia moved towards her daughter Wolf crouched down, his eyes soft as they looked gently into the small face in front of him.

'Bad dream?' It hurt her unbearably to see him like that, to understand what memories it must bring back to him of his own daughter, but as he held out his arms to Hannah and she climbed into them Lydia only saw a quiet tenderness in the hard male features that wrenched at her heart.

'You woke me up.' Hannah spoke fearlessly into the dark, handsome face in front of her. 'You're very noisy.'

'I'm sorry.' His face was rueful as he glanced at Lydia over her daughter's fair head.

'That's all right.' Hannah snuggled contentedly in his arms. 'I like you. I asked my mummy when you were coming to see us again,' she continued happily.

'And what did your mummy say?' he murmured quietly.

'She said you were too busy.' Hannah moved back an inch and surveyed him thoughtfully. 'But you aren't, are you?'

'No.' He smiled suddenly. 'I'm not at all busy, Hannah. Now...' He glanced at Lydia again, his eyes enquiring. 'If I'm the one who woke you up, how about if I put you back to bed—yes?'

'Yes, please.' Hannah was clearly enchanted by the thought, brown eyes dark with satisfaction.

'Perhaps your mummy will make me a cup of coffee while I do so?' Lydia nodded weakly. This was all too much. Wolf here in her small home, acting as though he had always been here. Her heart jumped into her mouth. Acting as though he *liked* being here.

It was some ten minutes later before she heard his footsteps on the stairs and she had no premonition of what was coming. She turned as he entered the room and then shrank back against the wall as she saw his face.

'Why, Lydia?' His voice was a low snarl and the dark colour burning the high cheekbones spoke of furious, contained rage. 'Why the fairy-tale?'

'What?' And then she realised, far, far too late, what Hannah had innocently revealed to the big, powerful man in front of her.

'He's dead, isn't he? He's been dead years.' His voice was raw and brutal and savage. 'I've suffered the tor-

ments of the damned for weeks, called myself every kind
of swine for my baser urges regarding you, and all the
time...' He was breathing hard and deep. 'I was burning
up inside for days when you first came to work for me,
and that day in the lift...' He shook his head angrily.
'I loathed myself afterwards, couldn't believe I'd fallen
so hard, and then when I found out he'd left you, that
there was a chance you were free——'

'I wanted to explain,' she said desperately. 'I
tried——'

'But not *too* hard.' The icy, cynical voice was scathing.
'It gave you some sort of kick, did it? To see me making
a total fool of myself?'

'It wasn't like that——'

'Who else knows?' He glared at her furiously. 'Mike,
of course, he'd just love this. And the typing-pool? And
the cleaners?'

'No, believe me, Wolf, it's not like that. I didn't try
to make you look a fool——'

'But you succeeded.' His voice was as hard as steel,
the man who had been in the room ten minutes before
now seeming a figment of her imagination. 'For the first
time in years I wanted to be with someone because of
who they were, or who I thought they were,' he finished
cuttingly. 'And however I tried to fight it the feeling got
stronger and stronger. But you were so naïve, so pure,
so untouchable.' The harsh bark didn't resemble a laugh
in any way. 'Oh, you're good, baby, I have to give you
that. You're the best.' He raked his hand through his
hair wildly, his eyes narrowed slits of cold ice. This was
worse than anything she could have imagined. She stared
at him with great bruised eyes as he verbally ripped
her apart.

'How long was the charade going to continue?' he asked icily. 'I knew I should have followed my head and not my heart after I'd seen you with Mike that day. It was all too pat, too convenient. And I *heard* him warning you to keep quiet! Hell, I don't believe all this! You dared to lecture me on my lifestyle when all the time——'

'It wasn't like that. You're making it sound as if I planned it all,' she protested desperately.

'Oh, and it just happened?' he asked bitterly. 'You told me a pack of lies, Lydia, admit it.'

'But——'

'Admit it,' he said ruthlessly.

'Yes, I lied.' She stared at him wildly, her eyes hunted. 'But Mike is nothing to do with this, I hardly know him. I lied to get the job and it didn't seem important at first. Not at first——'

'And later?' he asked grimly.

'Later...' Her voice trailed away. How could she explain later? How could she tell him that she had used her supposed husband as a defence against her own feelings for him and the attraction she knew he felt for her, albeit only physical? That she hadn't dared to let him know she was free because she would have been unable to resist him, but that in her case it wouldn't have just been a giving of her body. She would have given her mind, her soul, everything. She loved him. But he would have used her and walked away. *He would.* 'I knew you just wanted a brief affair,' she said bleakly.

'You knew?' He eyed her with such coldness that she felt the chill of it freeze her blood. 'The hell you did.'

'You told me you steered clear of any involvement, that you chose your women as much for that as anything else,' she said hotly. 'You can't deny that. You wanted physical satisfaction, maybe some fun——'

'Don't tell me what I wanted,' he growled furiously. 'So this is all my fault? Is that what you're saying?'

'No!' Her voice was too shrill, and she checked it quickly. Hannah arriving back on the scene would be the final straw. 'But you didn't tell me anything, *talk* to me——'

'I talked to you more than I've talked to anyone in years,' he said angrily. 'I felt as if I was treading on eggshells half the time but I tried——' He stopped abruptly. 'Hell, what am I defending myself for? Even if you'd dug a hole for yourself there were times you could have told me, you know that.'

'Yes, I know.' Her misery seemed to make him more angry.

'So why the hell didn't you? Because you liked having me on a string?' He eyed her coldly. 'Well?' he barked suddenly. 'Answer me.'

'What do you want me to say?' She knew she was losing the last thread of control but her temper had risen to match his. He was seeing this all his own way, he wasn't even trying to acknowledge the position he had put her in at the beginning of their relationship and, whatever he said, he *hadn't* talked to her, not really. If anyone had been kept at arm's length it was her! 'Just tell me and I'll say it. That's all you want, after all, isn't it—obedient little female puppets to jerk to your string? The great Wolf Strade, cold and unapproachable, making everyone tremble if they come within a hundred yards of you! You don't know the meaning of love and commitment and normal life. You're so caught up in your own little world. You talk about poor Elda being obsessed? Well, at least she is obsessed with something positive, a desire for her own child with the man she loves. You're just obsessed with emptiness——'

'Have you quite finished?' He was glaring at her, hands folded across his chest and his big body as taut as an iron rod.

'No.' She stared back defiantly, but the rage was beginning to die and a wave of agony take its place. This was the death-knell of all her secret hopes and desires. He would never forgive her for the things she had said, even if he could have forgiven her for the lies and deceit regarding Matthew. 'It's about time you listened to someone else for a change.'

'Is it, indeed?' The rigid control was slipping, she could see it in the burning fury in the piercing blue eyes. 'But perhaps I don't want to listen to you, Lydia, perhaps I want to do something quite different.'

'Don't you come near me.' As he took a step towards her she backed away, her hand to her mouth.

'Don't come near you?' He laughed bitterly. 'But why shouldn't I? You aren't a distressed young wife, forsaken by her childhood sweetheart, are you? Far from it.' He seemed beside himself with rage. 'What *exactly* you are I haven't the faintest idea and frankly I don't care. You are here now and so am I. That's all that matters.'

He walked back to the door and shut it, sliding a chair against it before turning and walking over to her again. She was standing straight and erect now, determined not to flinch before him. 'If I start to make love to you it won't be rape, you know that.' His face was hard and cold as he surveyed her insolently from head to toe, his eyes burning into her flesh wherever they touched. 'You want me, Lydia, you can't deny that.' She had given his pride a body-blow, she reflected silently as she saw the mask of arrogant hauteur that clothed the handsome, harsh features. 'I've waited longer for you than I've ever waited for a woman before, and enough is enough.'

If he took her like this, by force, he would never forgive himself. The knowledge was there inside her. It would poison the rest of his life with an insidious toxic contamination that he wouldn't be able to overcome. He was a proud man but he wasn't sufficiently egocentric to excuse this outrage, once the furious rage and bitterness had died.

'Yes, I want you.' She faced him, trembling and soft now, her eyes holding his, open and bare. 'I want you because I love you, Wolf, and you're right, it wouldn't be rape.'

'You love me?' He shook his head angrily, his voice gritty. 'I've been told that before too.'

'I don't doubt it.' She stared back at him, conscious that she was laying herself wide open to the worst sort of pain and rejection. 'But not by me. I do love you, whether you believe it or not,' she said quietly.

'I don't.' But his eyes were stricken as they held hers. 'I don't believe love is an emotion that really exists.'

'Yes, you do,' she said softly.

'No.' He shook his head blindly, his eyes hardening. 'Sex, lust, desire, those things are real and powerful and honest. You can dress them up as love but the end result is the same.'

'Which is?'

'This.' His mouth was angry and harsh as it ravaged hers, his arms like bands of steel as he held her so closely into his hard frame that she could feel his heart pounding like a sledge-hammer against the wall of his chest. She didn't try to fight him, she was intuitive enough to know that any movement of her body would send them over

...e edge into brutal passion, and she had to convince
...im that her feeling for him was more than blind desire.
He probably wouldn't, couldn't, accept her love for him,
but he had to know that in that alone she was different
from all the rest. If she succumbed now, gave in to the
fiery heat and sweet sensation that his nearness produced,
she would become just another name in his little black
book. But it was hard, doubly so because she had no
inner conviction that she could penetrate that cold, dark,
outer shell to the real man she had glimpsed fleetingly.
Maybe, if she hadn't lied, if he had taken the step of
trusting her...?

The feel and taste and intoxicating smell of him was
becoming more than she could deny. She felt a moment's panic at her weakness, at the vulnerability her
love for him had exposed. He would explain away her
response as animal desire, she knew that, but it was becoming harder to remain cold and unresponsive in his
arms.

His mouth had become more coaxing now, per-
suasive, moving to her throat and still lower in burning-
hot, feathery kisses that lit little chills of fire wherever
they touched. She moaned slightly, the sound escaping
her lips in spite of herself, and heard a low growl of
answering passion in the big body trapping hers. He was
hugely aroused against her softness, his mouth ravaging
the soft silky swell of her breasts as her blouse fell open
under his insistent fingers.

She wasn't going to be able to stop this. As her hands
moved up to his back, the hard swell of powerful muscles
clenching as he felt her touch, she knew she was lost.
She loved him too much...

The thought brought a little sob to her lips. Too much
to reach him. She began to shake helplessly, the know-

ledge that she had capitulated swept away by a feverish hunger to become as one with this strange, cold man who had captured her heart and her mind and turned her body into liquid heat. 'My love, my love...' She wasn't aware she had murmured out loud, wasn't aware of the tears dampening her face, but suddenly he pushed her from him with a groan that seemed wrenched out of the very depths of his body, and as she sank to the carpet, her legs refusing to support her, he stepped back a pace as though from something repugnant.

'You see?' He was panting hard, his face dark and ravaged by an emotion that caused the breath to constrict in her throat. He hated her. He was looking at her as though he hated her. 'Do you?' he demanded savagely. 'It all comes down to this, nothing more. You're no different from the rest.'

She stared up at him silently, her eyes wide and luminous like the beautiful eyes of a wounded doe.

'You lied to me.' The words were torn out of him. 'I don't know who you are.'

'I'm sorry——'

'And that make. it better?' He glared at her ruthlessly. 'Sex is the only real thing between a man and a woman and I'm going to prove that to you now.'

'No.' Her voice was very soft. 'If we make love it will be just that on my side, Wolf, love. From almost the first day of meeting you I couldn't understand why I felt like I did. I fought it, I admit it. I felt I'd betrayed Matthew, let him down in the worst way possible because what I'd felt for him didn't even begin to compare with the emotions you called forth. I called it physical desire too.' She stared at him, a touch of bitterness in her face now. 'But it is much, much more than that with me. I know you're incapable of loving a woman again, but it doesn't seem to make any difference. I can't kill this feeling however much I try.'

'You loved Matthew——'

'Yes, I did.' She raised her chin slightly, unaware that her blouse was still open, her body revealed in all its softness, and that the gesture of brave confrontation combined with the vulnerability her body presented hit him like a physical blow, causing his face to whiten.

'I loved him very much, but not in the way I love you. The love I had for him was undemanding, gentle. He'd always been there and I think we both misunderstood what we felt. He was an only child and so was I. Our love was more that of siblings, brother and sister, but neither of us realised it.'

'You expect me to believe that?' he bit out harshly.

'No.' She held his glance painfully. 'I don't suppose you'll believe anything I say.'

'Dead right.' His eyes narrowed on her face. 'Hell, you aren't worth this.' His voice cracked and he turned on his heel in the same instant, flinging the chair aside with a viciousness that frightened her and banging the door behind him as he strode into the dark street.

It was some time before the stillness of the house reached her bruised, aching senses, but then she rose slowly from the floor, her movements dull and sluggish and her face as white as a sheet. The tears had gone, burnt up in the fierce pain that had cauterised her mind so that all that was left was a numb, anaesthetising blankness. She had told him, laid her heart bare before him, exposed her love in all its fragility, and he had ground it under his heel.

She locked the front door automatically, her limbs heavy and leaden and her mouth swollen and bruised with the evidence of his lovemaking, and climbed the

stairs slowly, her movements automatic. She had ru...
everything, any chance they might have had. It was ...
her fault.

Mercifully sleep came immediately—a thick, empty
blanket in which there was no feeling, no pulse, no life.

CHAPTER NINE

WHEN Lydia awoke to the insistent ringing of the alarm the next morning the merciful covering had been lifted and the wound was exposed in all its raw agony. Somehow she got Hannah to nursery, returning home in a daze of pain and grief to an endless post-mortem that produced nothing but guilt and regret.

She *had* lied to him. She shut her eyes tightly in an agony of remorse. Knowing that it was the one thing he wouldn't tolerate. And what a lie. She shook her head desperately against the sight of his face in those last few moments before he had left. There was nothing she could do, no way back. It was the ultimate betrayal.

The hours slipped by somehow; she was hardly aware of their passing although she forced herself to eat a sandwich and drink a cup of coffee at lunchtime. She couldn't afford to indulge her misery at the cost of Hannah's peace of mind, and if she became ill it would only be her daughter who would suffer.

She paced endlessly up and down the small lounge after lunch. Tiger had made one or two tentative attempts to sit on her lap in the morning, but had now retired under the settee for sanctuary, watching her carefully with big saucer-wide eyes, clearly thinking she had gone mad. She couldn't blame him. She hadn't been reasoning like a sane woman lately. Why, oh, why hadn't she told Wolf about Matthew long before this? There had been so many opportunities...

170

She stifled a sob as she drove her fist into her mouth with a hard groan. And all this with Mike. He had obviously suspected she was in league with Anna's husband, at least initially. She should have given him a straightforward explanation after that very first incident, but she had been so horribly embarrassed it had been easier to push it to the back of her mind. 'Coward, coward, coward...' She looked out of the window bleakly. She wouldn't have thought a human heart could stand pain like this and not shatter.

Her mother phoned at two, her voice anxious. 'Lydia? Are you ill, darling? I phoned your office to see how Hannah liked her present, but there was another woman there. What's wrong?'

So he hadn't wasted any time in securing her replacement. Her heart jerked and thudded painfully. He hadn't even waited to see if she would go back. She clenched her teeth against the anguish. But of course he had known she wouldn't go back—how could she after the things they had said to each other?

'I'm OK, Mum, just seem to have gone down with one of these viruses.' She spoke carefully, making her voice as blank as she could. 'Not enough to knock me off my feet but enough to make concentrating at a word processor impossible.'

'Do you want me to come round? Fetch Hannah? Anything?'

'No, no, thanks. Everything's under control. A few days at home and I'll be fine, and I don't want you to catch anything.' She forced a modicum of warmth into her voice. 'Forty-eight hours and I'll be as right as rain.' As right as rain? What a stupid banality, she thought bitterly.

'Are you sure?' Her mother was unusually persistent. 'I'm not stupid, Lydia, and I *am* your mother. It isn't anything to do with that man, is it? Wolf Strade?'

'That man'? For a moment Lydia felt a flood of wild hysterical laughter well up inside. 'That man' had effectively battered through all her defences and shattered the self-esteem of the last few years into fragments. It was *everything* to do with him. And still she loved him more than life. She took a deep breath. 'No, of course not.' There was a pregnant silence on the other end of the phone that lengthened. It was an attribute of her mother's that she could be scathingly disbelieving without saying a word. 'Well, perhaps it is, but I can't talk about it now. Another time,' she added desperately.

'You know best.' Her mother's voice was disapproving but resigned. 'Well, if you're sure I can't help in any way... Give me a call if you change your mind.'

'I will. Thanks, Mum.'

'Goodbye, Lydia.'

'You know best.' Her mother's words taunted her after she had replaced the receiver. But she didn't, did she? She didn't know anything any more.

She thought about how he had come to the house, his explanation regarding Elda. So he was free... at the moment. Perhaps it would have been better to take the brief affair he had wanted? At least that way she would have had memories, if nothing else. Now there was just an empty void where her heart should have been.

And Wolf? Her heart thudded as she pictured him in his office, barking orders at the new secretary and immersed in work as usual. It wouldn't take him long to forget she even existed—if he still remembered, that was.

She ignored the doorbell at first. She needed time to pull herself together before she collected Hannah, and a door-to-door salesman was the last person she felt like coping with right now. They were renowned in this district and normally she could remain polite and firm, but today she wouldn't be responsible for her actions if they tried a hard sell. In fact the urge to bite and scream and kick at something, anything, was shockingly fierce. But they were persistent. She'd give them that. After a full minute of the bell ringing, with the sort of offensive determination that hit a raw spot deep inside, she suddenly leapt up and flew to the door, wrenching it open with a ferocious scowl that froze as Wolf removed his hand from the button.

'Hello.' He made no attempt to move.

'Hello.' She didn't either.

They stared at each other in silence for taut seconds before she forced words through her numb lips. 'I thought you were at the office.' It was inane, but his appearance following so closely behind her thoughts was shattering.

'The office?' She could have said the moon from the blankness in his deep voice. 'No. I haven't been to the office today.'

'Oh.'

He looked terrible. And gorgeous. He hadn't shaved and the black shadow on his chin gave a whole new meaning to the attraction of designer stubble. A flood of emotion surged into her chest, constricting breath and sending red-hot tears pricking painfully behind her eyelids. She stepped back quickly, petrified he'd notice. He hated emotion, she knew that.

'I——' He cleared his throat and tried again. 'I would like to come in, but if you don't want me to I understand. I guess after last night I'm the last person in the world you want to see.'

Wrong, wrong, wrong, she thought dazedly. Utterly and totally wrong. 'You look as if you could do with a coffee,' she said weakly as she waved him into the house.

'No. It's not coffee I need.' He followed her as far as the lounge doorway and then stood leaning against it, hands thrust deeply into his pockets and his eyes narrowed and piercingly blue as he watched her turn round and face him.

He was everything she had ever wanted in a man. The knowledge pierced her soul with fire. And he could have been hers, for a time at least, but she had thrown it all away. Her throat felt like sandpaper and she knew in a minute she was going to burst into tears, which would probably be the final straw for him. She didn't know why he was here but she did know emotional scenes weren't his style.

'What I *need* is to talk to you, explain——' He stopped abruptly and she knew the words weren't coming easily to him, that he found this baring of his soul distasteful.

'It's all right——'

'No, it's *not* all right!' The rigid control faltered and slipped, and for a moment the harsh intensity that flared in the tormented blue eyes caused her breath to stop. 'Dammit! It's anything but.'

He took a long deep pull of air but the mask was severely out of place now, his face naked and open for the first time she could remember. However could she have imagined he was unemotional? she asked herself faintly as fierce hunger, anger and burning contempt washed over his face in scorching savagery. He must hate her. To look at her like this he must hate her.

She backed from him, her hand to her mouth and her eyes wide with a painful suffering she couldn't hide. 'Please go. This won't do any good——'

'I'm not going to hurt you.' He swore softly as he saw the agony in her face. 'Dammit, Lydia, stop looking at me like that. I have to explain to you, you have to understand at least.'

'I do.' She forced herself to walk as far as the settee and sank down on it, her legs trembling. 'I know I lied to you and you must hate me for it, but please, I can't take much more——'

'But you have to understand *why*——'

'I don't care why!' Suddenly she was screaming at him as her nerves finally snapped. 'I don't care, do you hear? You think I'm deceitful and treacherous and dishonest, you've told me that. You think I wanted to make a fool of——' The lump of lead in her chest choked her voice, and as he made a move towards her she shot bolt-upright, her eyes flashing and her face as white as a sheet. 'Don't you touch me. Don't you dare to touch me. And I'm not going to cry, so don't worry. I just want you to go.'

'No.' It was a small word but coated in steel. 'Not till I've talked to you, properly, without any dramatics.'

Dramatics? He dared to call this bitter grief that was tearing her apart 'dramatics'? His words acted like a deluge of icy water, restoring control and freezing her heart. 'Then talk,' she said flatly as she faced him with her hands clenched into fists at her side. 'If that's what you want.'

'It is.' He shook his head slightly, although his eyes never left hers. 'I've got no right to be here, I know that, not after last night and the things I said, but I need to explain things just once before I get out of your life for good.'

She sat down then. The thought of Wolf being out of her life for good took her legs from under her.

'I was going to talk to you in Scotland but——' He stopped abruptly.

'But?' she asked wearily.

'But I chickened out, lost my nerve.' She stared at him, her eyes portraying her shock, and he laughed harshly, the sound a low, raw wound of pain and contempt. 'Surprised? I don't blame you. Doesn't quite fit in with the macho image, does it? The wolf who walks alone?' The self-derision was so scathingly bitter she could only watch him numbly as he began to pace the room, his hands clenching and unclenching at his sides.

'I told you my wife and child died eight years ago,' he said harshly, 'but there was something else, something I didn't tell you. They were killed on an icy country road driving into town to see a pantomime just before Christmas. An articulated lorry jack-knifed on a patch of black ice and they were killed instantly.'

'Wolf——' He raised his hand at her anguished voice, and now she saw his eyes were steady.

'The reason they were there, the reason they died all alone in a piece of twisted metal, was because I had a big contract going through that I considered more important than my family,' he continued tightly. 'I had arranged to be home in time to take them myself, but when a few problems delayed things I rang Miranda and told her to take Carrie in her car and I'd meet her there. I left nearly half an hour later. I knew I'd miss the first part, but what the hell? It was only a two-bit pantomime, wasn't it? No influential contacts present, no high-fliers to clinch a deal with.' The pain and disgust in his voice were almost more than she could bear. She was seeing the real Wolf now, the man behind the mask, and it was agonising.

'I saw the police cars first, then a fire engine and a couple of ambulances...' His eyes focused on her, black with pain. 'There was nothing anyone could do. The car was mangled beyond recognition but, in one of those quirks of fate, the number-plate had been ripped off and was found intact at the side of the road. Funny thing...' He stared at her blindly. 'I couldn't believe it when the policeman told me the number, and yet I'd known the first moment I saw the road was blocked. I'd known.'

'But you didn't know the accident was going to happen,' she said softly as the tears streamed down her face. 'It was a million to one chance, one of those things against which there would have been no protection even if you had been driving. You do see that, don't you?'

'Maybe.' He raked back his hair savagely. 'Maybe not, we'll never know.' He continued the pacing again, his face grey. 'After the funeral I guess I went crazy for a time. I sure can't remember much about the weeks that followed, anyway. I think they're blanked forever. Dad came over and took me off somewhere, a log cabin in the depths of the Lake District with the snow up to the windows. I think he saved my sanity.' He stopped and turned to her, his eyes focusing on her white face. 'And then one day I wanted to go back. The house was weird, empty, and I began to sort Miranda's things—it was as if it was happening in a film to someone else. But I couldn't go into Carrie's room.' He stopped and she saw moisture glitter bright for a moment in the vivid blue eyes before it was blinked harshly away. 'I never did go into her room again, perhaps I should have. Anyway...' He continued the pacing again, his big body seeming to fill the small room, 'I found letters, addresses, even little gifts among Miranda's things. She'd been having a string of affairs from the first year we were married, before too, maybe. I don't know. Some of the letters were...disgustingly intimate. I sat and read them all, every one, and then I left the house and never went back. I had the site bulldozed within weeks.' He laughed harshly, the sound raw in the stillness. 'Half a million lost in a futile gesture, but I didn't care. I still don't.'

He stopped, turning to look out of the window with his back towards her. 'I couldn't believe I'd lived with someone, shared my life and my bed with them, and not known them. None of it had been real—the love, the sharing, the laughter. Oh, we used to have rows, mainly about my work, which I could understand. She was frustrated being at home with a child and I wasn't home enough—the isolation used to drive her mad.'

She waited, hardly daring to breathe as he paused. 'The worst thing, the worst thing of all was that I couldn't let myself think of Carrie for a time after that. She and Miranda were somehow linked together and I had to blank them both to survive. It got better...' He turned to face her now, taking a deep hard breath. 'It had to,' he said simply.

She rose slowly and walked over to him, putting her small hands against his chest as she looked up into his ravaged face. 'I don't know what to say,' she said softly. 'I thought it was bad with Matthew, the grief, the anger, but I couldn't have got through what you did.'

'Yes, you would have done.' He had tensed at her touch but made no effort to touch her, his body taut and still as he looked down at her. 'You've got more guts than any other lady I know.'

'Wolf——'

'You've got to hear it all, Lydia.' He moved away as though her close proximity hurt him, and she stood bereft, her heart thudding. Was he going to tell her all this and then leave? He was capable of it, she knew that, and she had no idea where all this was leading.

'I was in a mess for a long, long time, poison to myself and everyone else,' he continued grimly. 'Truth became an obsession with me, as did the conviction that I could never trust another woman—they were good for one thing and one thing only.' She flinched and he nodded slowly. 'That's how it was, Lydia, I'm not going to dress it up with fancy words and phrases. I had affairs with women who knew the score, were free and wanted a good time. There are plenty about,' he added cynically. 'Then one day a blonde fireball stormed into my office and put me in my place more effectively than it has ever been done before.'

'It's been done before?' she asked, in a voice she had trouble keeping steady.

'Well, no...' His face relaxed for a moment. 'I've never been any good at taking criticism, believe it or not.'

'I do.' She didn't know if she could take much more of this without breaking down completely, she really didn't.

'And I thought, this one actually says it as it is.' His voice held the note of amazement he must have felt at the time. 'No beating about the bush, no flannel, straight for the jugular. And then...' He stopped now and his eyes held hers steadily. 'And then I came into the office and found you in a huddle with the guy I *knew* was pulling a fast one.'

'Mike was——'

'No, I don't want to know.' He held her glance firmly. 'Whatever it is, I know you weren't involved with him now.'

'How?' she asked faintly.

'Because last night I walked the streets for hours and finally listened to my heart for the first time in years,' he said slowly. 'I used to do it all the time once, before——' He stopped. 'And then I lost the knack——'

'Whether you want to hear it or not, Mike is the husband of a close friend of mine,' she said quickly as he paused for breath. 'I'd forgotten he worked for you and then he came in the office and asked me to keep quiet about it, said you didn't like your secretary to be friendly with the other employees——'

'He's a cute one.' He looked at her wryly. 'And you were worried how he'd survive after he left my employ? The guy will be the next prime minister.'

'Wolf, I'm so sorry——'

'I love you, Lydia.' There was all the emotion she could ever have wanted in his face, and as her heart began thudding she watched the ice-blue eyes mist over. 'I mean I *really* love you. Not a for-the-time-being love. I've loved you from the minute I set eyes on you, can you believe that?' he asked, with a shred of desperation in his voice.

She tried to smile, but as her mouth quivered he moved across the short space separating them and pulled her into him, his body shaking almost as violently as hers.

'I don't deserve to ask but I'm going to anyway. Last night—last night you told me you cared. Have I destroyed that? Can you forgive me?'

'Me forgive you?' Her voice was muffled against his hard chest but it felt so good, so good, she would never have believed how good. 'But I've lied to you, it was all my fault——'

'No.' He moved her into the circle of his arms, staring down at her mouth. 'I put you in an impossible position from the word go, I realised that last night as I roamed the city. You have Hannah to support, this house... What the hell were you supposed to do?'

'But I shouldn't have lied.' She stared up at him weakly. 'And you were right, there were lots of times I could have told you about Matthew——'

'I don't care about Matthew.' His hand traced the line of her lips as his eyes devoured her. 'I don't care about any damn thing except you. I treated you badly when you first came to work for me, I know that, but I was despising myself for the way I felt when I knew you were married, and I wasn't sure how Mike fitted into the scheme of things. I wanted you, you'll never know how much I wanted you. The number of times I wanted to lay you out on that office floor——' He shut his eyes for a second. 'And I kept telling myself it was a physical hunger, nothing more, nothing unusual. I was angry you were married, but relieved too. It took the ball out of my court—*fait accompli*.'

She was still holding back, she didn't know why. It was too much, she couldn't take it in. He loved her? But all the time he had been so cold, so aloof...

'And then I found out he'd left. It scared the hell out of me. I didn't sleep for nights. I knew a brief affair wasn't possible, you weren't that sort of woman and my feelings were too deep and dangerous for that anyway, but if I let you in, just the tiniest bit, I was vulnerable again like the rest of the suckers out there. I couldn't take it, Lydia.'

'But you were so cold, so full of contempt,' she murmured softly. She wanted to believe him, oh, she did, but after what he'd been through, how did he *know* this was real for him?

'Aimed mainly at myself,' he said grimly as though he could read her mind. 'I tried to keep you at a distance but it wasn't working. You were everything I wanted in a woman—soft, gentle, innocent, and yet with a determination and an honesty that——'

'Don't.' She flinched at the last words, her face changing.

'You are honest, Lydia.' He cupped her face in his hands. 'I want to kiss you, but if I do I shan't be able to think any more, to convince you, and I need to convince you, don't I? I can see it in your eyes. Have I hurt you too much? I tried to convince myself yesterday that I needn't take the cataclysmic step, that you were just like Miranda, saying one thing and living a lie. But I couldn't. I've never loved anyone like I love you and I never shall again. You have my heart, Lydia. It isn't much of a gift and you deserve better, but it is wholly yours.'

'Kiss me.' She reached up to him, her heart in her eyes. 'Kiss me. I don't want to talk any more.'

'Lydia...' His voice was a groan, and as he took her mouth she became mindless beneath his, her body fluid and soft as his hands moved down her body in a passionate caress. Her arms clung round his neck as they swayed together in an agony of love, their mouths fusing in an endless kiss that was pure sensation. 'I love you, Lydia, for pity's sake say you'll marry me. Nothing else will do. I want to love you, take care of you, protect you, be a father to Hannah. I want everything, all of it, all of you. Hell——' he moved her slightly from him to look into her starry eyes '—say something, woman, you're torturing me.'

'Love me.' She breathed in the smell of him as she clung to the hard-muscled body, her mind spinning. 'Love me now.'

'No.' He moved her to arm's length now, his eyes steady. 'I want an answer in cold blood, not the heat of the moment. I want to hear you say you love me.'

'I do.' She stared at his dark, handsome face as her head cleared, and then drew back a little, a touching uncertainty in her face. This was too sudden. Too great a change-about. 'What if you change your mind, if it begins to go wrong?' she asked faintly.

'Do you love me?' he persisted grimly.

'More than life.'

'Then we'll discuss it going wrong on our twenty-fifth wedding anniversary,' he said, his voice thick now as his hand traced one swollen nipple through the soft silk of her blouse. 'That should give us enough time to consider if we've done the right thing.'

And then there was nothing but fiery, heady pleasure as his mouth fastened on hers again, the kiss deepening to a primitive assault on her senses that was an act of possession in itself. She moaned softly in her throat, lost in a mounting exultation that he loved her. *He loved her.*

EPILOGUE

'WELL, Mrs Strade?' Lydia stretched languorously as a possessive, skilled hand stroked her dreamily out of sleep before it settled on one firm, full breast as its partner continued its erotic assault on her body. 'Fifteen years to go.'

'What?' She opened drowsy eyes to find Wolf propped on one elbow as he surveyed her through those silver-blue eyes that she had once imagined were as cold as ice. There was fire beneath the ice, she knew that now, and she also knew it was just for her.

He moved slightly, pulling her more beneath him, and as she felt one hard-muscled leg on hers, the body-hair furry against her softness, her body responded as it always did. 'Only another fifteen years to go before you tell me if I'm to get my marching orders.' The hard, chiselled face was tender and warm as he looked down into her sleep-flushed face, and the curling hair on his chest tickled her breasts as he bent to deposit a swift kiss on her mouth before resuming his original position. 'Don't tell me you've forgotten this is our tenth wedding-anniversary?' he asked softly.

'Of course I haven't.' Her indignation was lost under his mouth as it swooped down in hard passion now and took possession of hers, turning her bones to water as it did its devastating work on her senses.

'You're nice to wake up to, Mrs Strade.' He ran a slow, satisfied finger over her curves, leaving a trail of fire in its wake. 'And nice to go to sleep with, and nice——'

'Oh, you!' She flicked him laughingly on one muscled shoulder as she thought again how lucky she was to have this man for her own.

'And you adore me, don't you...?' He kissed her throat lingeringly. 'So I'll take my present now.' He raised his head again and looked down into her flushed face, his eyes hot and the firm mouth she had thought so severe smiling with sensual anticipation. She shivered delightedly.

'Your present?' She arched provocatively beneath him, deliberately misunderstanding him. 'I might not have bought you a present.'

'Oh, you have.' He drew back the dark red sheet and feasted his eyes on her pale, slim body spread out to his gaze. 'And it's tasty, very tasty.'

'Wolf...' She giggled as he eyed her wickedly, his mouth curving in the boyish grin that was so at odds with the hard, male face. 'What about the children? I have to——'

'You don't have to do anything but please me.' The arrogance was intentional and satisfied. 'You know how Hannah enjoys the infants—let her have her moment of fun with them before the day begins.'

'But——' The protest was lost as he drew her against him, the feel of his magnificent body sending all lucid thought out of her head. It still amazed her, this passion that was a white-hot flame every time he touched her. Playful, tender, fierce, lusty—however he made love to her the result was the same, a total melting of her body in a wave of overwhelming pleasure that left no room for anything else.

She wouldn't have believed a man's body could work such magic on her senses, but since that very first time, when he had possessed her so completely the rest of the world had shattered into a million pieces, the mere feel of him was enough to set her body tingling. He was a devastating lover. She opened her eyes now as his dark head bent to her breasts, their peaks already swollen and ripe in anticipation of his caress.

And an incredible father. James had been born five years after their marriage—Wolf had insisted he wanted a few years to enjoy her and get to know Hannah before they had children of their own—with Edward following a year later and little Jane Carrie eighteen months after that.

He had never shown any partiality towards his own children at the cost of Hannah, indeed he seemed to have a special relationship with Matthew's daughter that his own children couldn't touch. Hannah had healed his stark grief over his first daughter in a way Lydia could never have hoped to do, accepting Wolf totally from the first moment and showering him with childish love and affection, clearly delighted with her 'new daddy'. She was nearly fourteen now and breathtakingly lovely, and the other children adored their big sister as she did them.

'Wolf?' She raised his head upwards as she slid down the bed a little to meet his face. 'I have got a present for you, you know.'

'As I expected, wench.' He took the delay in their lovemaking with indulgent good humour, knowing she wouldn't be able to resist him for long.

'I'm just not sure if you'll really like it.' She was still holding his face, wedged as she was under his body, and he smiled slowly, his eyes slumberous.

'I'll like it.' He moved his body slightly and she gasped with pleasure. 'Well?' He moved on to his elbows and looked down at her, his eyes narrowed.

'The thing is, I've given you similar ones before.'

'You have?'

'But this is a little different.' He smiled at her teasing and did something with his hands that had her breathing more quickly as shivers of sensation flickered over her body. 'It comes in pairs.'

'Pairs?' Now she had all his attention as he rolled to one side, his face straightening. 'You aren't saying...?'

'Twins.' She grinned at him happily. 'It was confirmed yesterday.'

'Twins.' He shut his eyes for a moment and then gave a laugh of sheer delight. 'Twins.' He sat up in the bed looking ridiculously pleased with himself before his expression altered. 'And you're all right?' She loved him for the immediate concern.

'Of course.' She placed a satisfied hand over the faint mound of her stomach. 'Or I will be when you give me *my* present.'

'I'll just get it——' As he went to move from the bed she caught his arm indignantly. 'Wolf!'

'You know I love you?' He fell back against her with a low chuckle. 'Really love you?' Now his eyes were serious and his mouth was tender with something that caught at her heartstrings. 'You are my sun, moon and stars, my darling, the air I breathe and my life-blood...'

'As you are minc.'

He took her mouth in a long, passionate kiss that awakened both their bodies anew to the delights to come, and then, as his mouth began an erotic downward spiral over her satin-smooth flesh, she shut her eyes as she murmured his name.

'My darling, my own Wolf...'

And then words weren't necessary as he took her with him into the heights.

MILLS & BOON

Mills & Boon are proud to bring you **Sally Wentworth's** glittering new three part series—*Ties of Passion*.

Each book within the Romance series, follows a different member of the Brodey clan—a wealthy vintner family—in their search for love.

Look out for the following titles:

Chris in September 1995

Francesca in October 1995

Calum in November 1995

Money, looks, style—the Brodey family have everything... except love

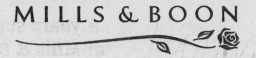

MILLS & BOON

Next Month's Romances

Each month you can choose from a wide variety of romance with Mills & Boon. Below are the new titles to look out for next month.

A years supply of Mills & Boon romances — absolutely free!

Would you like to win a years supply of heartwarming and passionate romances? Well, you can and they're FREE! All you have to do is complete the word puzzle below and send it to us by 29th February 1996. The first 5 correct entries picked out of the bag after that date will win a years supply of Mills & Boon romances (six books every month—worth over £100). What could be easier?

GMWIMSIN

NNSAUT

ACEHB

EMSMUR

ANCOE

DNSA

RTOISTU

THEOL

ATYCH

NSU

MYSTERY DESTINATION

Please turn over for details on how to enter

How to enter

Simply sort out the jumbled letters to make ten words all to do with being on holiday. Enter your answers in the grid, then unscramble the letters in the shaded squares to find out our mystery holiday destination.

After you have completed the word puzzle and found our mystery destination, don't forget to fill in your name and address in the space provided below and return this page in an envelope (you don't need a stamp). Competition ends 29th February 1996.

Mills & Boon Romance Holiday Competition
FREEPOST
P.O. Box 344
Croydon
Surrey
CR9 9EL

Are you a Reader Service Subscriber?   Yes ❑   No ❑

Ms/Mrs/Miss/Mr _____

Address _____

_____

_____ Postcode _____

One application per household.

You may be mailed with other offers from other reputable companies as a result of this application. If you would prefer not to receive such offers, please tick box. ❑

mps
MAILING
PREFERENCE
SERVICE

COMP495
B